Ral's

Zorn Warriors - Book One

By Laurann Dohner

Ral's Woman by Laurann Dohner

Kidnapped from Earth by the Anzon, deemed useless by her captors, Ariel has become the prize in a brutal fight between vicious-looking aliens. And the winner is the biggest, scariest, most tempting alien of them all. In Ral's arms, Ariel will learn how truly carnal captivity can be.

Also kidnapped, and forced into slavery, warrior Ral is focused on freeing his fellow Zorn—until Ariel. The beautiful human woman consumes him, urging Ral to claim his prize in all ways. Now she's his to love, to cherish, to protect…even from those he'd never suspect.

Zorn Warrior Series

Ral's Woman

Kidnapping Casey

Tempting Rever

Berrr's Vow

Coto's Captive

Ral's Woman

Copyright © May 2016

Editor: Kelli Collins

Cover Art: Dar Albert

ISBN: 978-1-944526-19-1

ALL RIGHTS RESERVED. The unauthorized reproduction or distribution of this copyrighted work is illegal, except for the case of brief quotations in reviews and articles.

Criminal copyright infringement is investigated by the FBI and is punishable by up to 5 years in federal prison and a fine of $250,000.

All characters and events in this book are fictitious. Any resemblance to actual persons living or dead is coincidental.

Chapter One	7
Chapter Two	21
Chapter Three	34
Chapter Four	48
Chapter Five	59
Chapter Six	71
Chapter Seven	86
Chapter Eight	102
Chapter Nine	115
Chapter Ten	131

Chapter One

Ariel kept her eyes down. She'd learned not to look up.

Her left cheek hurt from the bruises she was sure marred her face. She knew help would never come. She was still in deep shock and it was harder and harder to function as the hours passed.

Her old life was over, changed forever, and death would probably greet her really soon. This couldn't be happening.

How many times had *that* thought crossed her mind in the days since she'd been taken?

Her gaze drifted around the cave floor. Someone had painstakingly swept up the dirt and debris until it was almost clean. There were lights along the ceiling so the room was well lit.

She heard shoes striking the stones, and fear gripped her. What now?

The thought barely surfaced before she heard one of the men who'd grabbed her enter the room.

"Useless," he said softly.

She lifted her gaze.

The man wasn't human. And the shock of someone *not* being human hadn't started to dim yet. Days ago, if someone had told her other races existed, she would have laughed and asked them what movie they had watched too much.

It wasn't funny anymore.

Her gaze swept the man's bluish pale skin and then dropped. His eyes were yellow. They were serpent-like, and his voice was wispy in a creepy way that sent bad chills down her spine.

"Did you hear me, Earthling? You're useless."

She nodded but didn't speak. She knew if she looked at him too long or if she spoke, it would warrant another blow to her face.

They were Anzons. That's what she'd been told when they had grabbed her from the woods by her home. The days she'd been held captive felt like forever.

Another set of footsteps. She glanced up. The females of their species had the same eerie yellow eyes and bluish skin tone. They had breasts and seemed to grow hair only in a strip, from the top of their heads to the lower part of their neck, but their body structure wasn't that different from their males. They were all lean and long.

"It has been confirmed," the woman said. "She's not capable of breeding with our men. Humans aren't the answer we seek."

"We could give the males some relief with her. She's not hideous to look at and her form is similar enough to ours."

The woman hissed loudly. "The physical examination I gave her when she was unconscious says otherwise. She'd die."

"She's useless anyway."

The woman frowned. "Where is your compassion, Yoz? It would be excruciating for her. The hard shell at the tip of your staff would tear her apart inside. She would bleed out, and the pain would be..." The woman shivered. "I wouldn't wish it upon even an enemy. We're not at war with her world."

"She'll die anyway...and I am curious."

"Yoz," the woman hissed. "I will not allow it. I have another purpose for her."

"We need a worker?"

"No. I thought we could award her to one of the miners. They probably aren't breeding compatible, but sexually, it wouldn't be harmful to hand her over to one of them."

It was Yoz's turn to hiss. "Vhal, that's disgusting. That's cruelty. They are so hideous!"

"But they wouldn't kill her. And they have hair like she has."

The man snorted. Ariel sensed his eyes on her. "She has little body hair. They have more. They are also much bigger. Their skin texture looks the same, though."

"I've already discussed this with Mon. He agreed. It is done. Take her to the mines now. Mon awaits her."

Fear struck Ariel deeply. She jerked her head up and locked her eyes on the woman. "What is going on? Please tell me something. Please!"

The man hissed angrily at Ariel. The woman—Vhal—gripped his arm and shook her head. Compassion filled her face as she released the man. Vhal walked forward, blinked at Ariel a few times, and ran a lizard-like tongue across her thin blue lips.

"You were taken from your planet as we passed because our males outnumber our females eighteen to one. We're facing eventual extinction if we don't find a race of females to breed with our men. Our female bodies only support one or two egg cycles in our lifetimes. We lay our eggs and hatch our young, and only have three to six children per egg cycle. We tested you, but you are not breeding compatible with our species."

Ariel was stunned. "May I please go home then?"

"I'm sorry, but no. We are on a large…" She frowned. "You would call it an asteroid. We send ships out to inhabited planets. We have already been to yours, and we're very careful with our fuel. Our mission is important and we must complete it before we're allowed to return to our home planet. If we do not find breed-compatible females, we will all eventually die of old age. It is imperative that we save our race. If we do find breeders, we will need all of our fuel to take them to our planet."

Hot tears filled Ariel's blue eyes. "So I'll never see my home again?"

"I'm sorry." The woman's hissing voice sounded sad. "We have workers who mine this asteroid to give us fuel and more living spaces. You will be awarded to one of them for his hard work. They are Zorn. It is another race of people we own."

Own? She hadn't missed that term. Dread filled Ariel. "What will happen to me?"

The woman blinked. "They treat the few females they have well. They do not share their females, so you will be awarded to just one of them. The language implant in your ear will allow you to communicate with the male you are given to. Our commander takes pleasure in sports, so he makes the miners compete. He offers them rewards. You will be a prize."

She stared up at the woman. "Please…no."

The woman nodded slowly. "It is better than what Yoz had in store for you. A sexual mating with one of my kind would kill you very painfully." The woman turned. "Take her, Yoz."

Ariel wanted to fight but she knew it would be useless. The man was six feet tall and very strong, though he was thin. He gripped the chain attached to her wrist. It had to be some kind of alien touch-release shackle because it unlocked from the wall when he gripped it.

He walked away, not waiting to see if Ariel would follow or not. She got to her feet to walk quickly after him so she wasn't dragged. The man had long legs. Their alien torsos weren't that long but their legs were much longer than human legs.

Yoz led her through stone corridors. She gasped when she saw a large window of what appeared to be thick glass. She stared beyond it into literal outer space, millions of stars in a black sea.

Yoz yanked hard on her chain and made her jerk forward. Pain shot up her arm.

"Beautiful," he hissed. "But stare at it later. You will see enough of it to be sick of it quickly. *I* am sick of it."

He led her to what looked sort of like an elevator but was more of a rounded tube. No walls were attached to the platform. Yoz gripped the back of her neck and held on.

The platform suddenly dropped out from under them at an alarming rate.

Fear gripped Ariel. She was pretty sure she would tear up her skin if she touched one of the rough rock walls as the floor dropped them lower into the bowels of the asteroid. The man grasping her didn't release her neck until the platform slowed to a stop. She saw more stone corridors.

Yoz walked off the platform. "Come fast. I am being called." The man touched his ear. "I am nearly there, Mon."

Ariel swallowed. She didn't see any kind of device on the man's ear, just skin. Then again, she'd touched her own ear many times since she'd woken up after being taken. She'd been so stunned by her surroundings at first that it had taken her hours to realize, when she was spoken to, the aliens' lips didn't move correctly to form the words she heard in her ear. And she only heard them in one ear, not the other. She'd been informed that they'd implanted something in one ear so she could understand their language.

Yoz must also have some kind of implanted communication device in his cone-shaped ear.

She saw a large door and Yoz stopped, putting his hand on it. Anzons had only four fingers, and didn't possess thumbs. The door groaned before it opened. Cooler air hit them both. Ariel shivered as it blasted them. Yoz just started walking.

"Hurry or the door will crush you," he hissed.

She ran to catch up with him, and at another loud groan, Ariel turned her head back in time to see the door slam down to the floor with a noisy thud. She flinched before returning her focus in front of her.

The halls were wider here, she noted—and then she heard something that sent fear up her spine again. It sounded like growling.

"It has already begun," Yoz hissed. Excitement made him speak faster.

They turned a corner and the ceiling disappeared. The corridor ended in a large cavern. She saw more of Yoz's kind standing on a wide walkway of sorts, all of them staring down at the cavern floor.

Yoz pushed through them and Ariel had little choice but to follow, since he'd once more grabbed her wrist leash. The bluish aliens stared at her as she walked past at least twenty of them. These ones wore thick black clothing that looked like hard shells, with weapons strapped around their waists.

Yoz moved toward a very tall alien. The male wore the black shell uniform, and had weapons attached around his waist as well. The alien turned his head and Ariel met a cold yellow gaze. The alien eyed her back as his scary stare wandered down her body. His gaze jerked to Yoz.

"Strip her down and chain her on the platform."

Yoz hesitated. "Everything?"

"Is she wearing anything under her clothing?"

"There are small coverings over her breasts and her sex chamber."

"Leave those on. I don't want a riot."

Yoz nodded and pulled Ariel out onto another walkway. It was a long strip of flooring without rails, ending in a round open platform similar to their version of an elevator. This one had two bars coming up from the floor. Yoz led her toward the platform and pointed to the center.

"Stand and hold."

She was afraid. "Hold?"

"Do not move. If you fall, you die."

She tried to peer over the platform to the ground, but Yoz gripped her throat to yank her head up as he pushed her to the center of the platform.

"Do as you are told."

She held still and kept her head up. He released her throat and yanked the leash upward to raise her arm, then touched the leash to one of the poles, where it instantly attached. He turned and Ariel's gaze followed him. Yoz held up his hand and another leash was thrown at him from one of the bluish aliens. He caught it easily and gripped Ariel's other wrist. He put the leash around it and once more jerked her arm up, attaching that leash to the second pole.

Ariel's arms were now above her, spread wide. She could stand, but could only move a few inches either way at most.

Yoz stepped in front of her to stare down into her frightened eyes. "I feel sorry for you."

She gasped when he gripped her shirt to tear at it roughly, helpless to stop the alien as the material was torn from her body. She stood there in a skirt and her bra, but not for long. He reached down to shove his fingers inside her skirt and his sharp fingernails shredded the waist of the garment from the inside out. He yanked the material from her body so Ariel was left standing in only her bikini briefs and bra.

Yoz eyed her with pity. Shaking his head, he walked away off the platform. Ariel turned her head to track him as he walked back across the walkway to his fellow aliens.

The platform she stood on suddenly dropped fast.

Ariel gasped at the falling sensation, fighting a scream. The platform came to a stop with a stomach-dropping lurch. She had probably descended fifty feet to the cavern floor in just a few seconds.

She couldn't help but gape at her surroundings.

She saw a group of about eighty aliens. They were definitely males. She was getting her first look at what must be the Zorn. They looked *huge*. And they had hair, all right, she thought, remembering that earlier comment from Vhal. The males had long, thick hair that ran down their backs to their waists. They had massive chests, on clear view because none of them wore shirts. They had dark brown skin, almost looking deeply tan, and huge muscles.

One stood in front of the rest, and Ariel stared at his face. He looked almost human. The only outward difference was his nose, which was flatter and wider than a human's. He had high cheekbones and full lips.

Then those lips opened and she saw sharp teeth.

Fear hit Ariel. Baring his teeth, the man looked like some kind of alien vampire. Her eyes locked on his fangs before she tore her gaze away to stare at another man who moved closer to the front.

The light caught this man's eyes. They were a bright, electric-blue. It was a color she'd never seen before on a living being. They almost glowed.

Terrified, Ariel started to breathe faster. The sounds around her slowly penetrated her terror and she heard the men growling like vicious animals. She closed her eyes. She fought the wrist restraints but to no avail; she couldn't get free of the leashes holding her arms above her.

"The winner takes her," a deep voice hissed from above. "I want fighting in fours. Clear the area and pick the fighters."

Ariel forced her eyes open. She didn't want to look but she had to. The growling had stopped and the men moved back, into the shadows. She couldn't see anything beyond the well lit area in front of her.

She took deep breaths, trying to calm down. These animalistic men were going to fight over her.

They looked positively savage. Would the winner eat her? Was she *dinner*?

She didn't know which was worse—the idea that they were fighting to eat her, or to have sex with her.

Four men walked out of the shadows. Ariel stared at them but they didn't look at her. They peered somewhere above.

"Begin," the deep male voice demanded.

The men split into pairs to attack each other. They used fists and feet. The sounds of flesh hitting flesh were loud, as were the growls and grunts as blows landed.

Before long, two men went down and the remaining pair turned on each other. One of the men landed a roundhouse kick that threw the other man out of the lit area. He didn't return.

The last man standing walked to the side of the fighting area. He waited, crossing his arms over his chest.

Four more men came out. The fighting began again.

Ariel flinched at the brutality of it. These men were not messing around. Blood splattered on the floor and she heard one man's arm break, the crack loud in the cavernous space. The man roared as he went down, holding his arm. Someone came from the shadows to drag him away. The man who'd won that match waited for the other pair to finish. When one of the pair remained, the two aliens attacked each other.

Ariel closed her eyes. She didn't want to watch any more. But she could hear it. The sounds of fighting went on and on, brutal noises, match after match, until finally silence filled her ears.

She opened her eyes in curiosity.

Large, muscular men were waiting on the sideline. Some of them were smeared with blood; a few eyed the others and backed away into the darkness to bow out of fighting. Ariel counted the remaining men who stood there waiting to fight. Sixteen.

"Begin," the voice ordered from above.

All sixteen moved into the lit area, fighting in groups together. Roars and growls erupted as they battled. The injured were dragged away into the shadows until it came down to three males. Two of them teamed together to attack the biggest one.

Ariel studied the lone man being attacked by the other two. He was a huge son of a bitch. He was bigger than his opponents by a few good inches and he looked thicker in the arms and shoulders. Despite his size, he fought with amazing speed as he dodged fists and feet. He punched one man in the face. Ariel heard something crack, and then the injured man went staggering back, collapsing to the floor. Blood covered the fallen man's face. He whimpered and rolled to his side to cover his face with both hands. He didn't get up.

Her gaze flew to the last two men fighting. The larger one swung out a foot and kicked the other man in the chest. He groaned as he hugged his ribs, dropping to his knees while blood dripped out of his mouth. His chin dropped to his chest before he crashed to the floor.

The lone man stood there, growling. He suddenly threw his head back, roaring out into the cavern. Ariel wished she could cover her ears so the terrifying noise could be muffled. The man's roar finally trailed off as he turned around to glare up at the bluish aliens.

"She's yours, Ral," the alien above her hissed. "Release her to him."

Ariel felt more terror as the man named Ral moved toward the platform. She heard something behind her, and one of the bluish men appeared on the walkway. When he reached her, he gripped her wrist and freed first one, then the other from the restraints.

Blood rushed back into her arms as she lowered them to her side, causing a pins-and-needles sensation. She gasped as the bluish man gripped her arms firmly. He shoved her forward until she found herself staring up a good foot and some inches into the face of the man who'd won her. He had to be six and a half feet tall, to her five-three.

She recognized him instantly from his eyes. Those bright, electric-blue eyes, that looked like they glowed, belonged to the man she'd seen before the fighting began. He was breathing hard now, and she saw sharp white fangs peeking from his full lips. His flattened nose twitched and a soft growl came from his throat.

His hands were large and warm as he gripped her hips. He tugged her from the platform, turning her toward the darkness of the cavern with a snarl.

Ariel's knees started to buckle. She would have crashed to the rock floor if the man's large hands weren't gripping her hard enough to hold her up. He spun her to face him, staring down at her.

"Mine," he growled.

Ariel opened her mouth but nothing came out. The man lifted her so they were face-to-face. She automatically put her hands on his chest so her upper body didn't slam into his, her flesh pale against his dark brown skin. She touched hard muscles covered by firm flesh, while staring into his eyes. He had long black eyelashes that matched his thick black mane of hair. His skin was hotter than hers by far.

"Mine," he growled softly at her.

Ariel gasped when he easily tossed her over his shoulder. A thickly muscled arm trapped her legs against his chest while a firm hand gripped her ass, holding her in place. He stormed away from the platform, into the darkness, where Ariel couldn't see a thing. So she just closed her eyes and fought the terror she was feeling.

What would he do to her?

Chapter Two

Ariel could smell him. The scent wasn't bad or unpleasant. He actually smelled good, considering he'd just been fighting. She realized he had smooth skin under the hair that fell to his waist. At first glance she'd thought the shiny hair grew from their backs as well, but it was all from his head, like a human's. It was softer to the touch than it looked.

She heard low growls as he walked quickly with her. At first it was so dark she couldn't see, but when faint light started to penetrate as he kept going, she could make out rough walls. The light grew brighter until she could see the floor. It was an uneven stone, not smooth like the hallways she'd seen above.

"You won," a voice growled softly. "Who will you give this one to, Ral?"

Ral stopped walking. "She is mine."

There was a pause. "But you always give away what you win. I have been waiting the longest."

"Not her," Ral growled. "This one is *mine*."

"But—"

"Enough!" Ral snarled. "Move or I'll move you."

She heard the other man growl. "Will you at least share her?"

"No."

That one word made Ariel feel relief. She didn't want to be shared.

The man holding her snarled again. "Move out of my way. If you wanted a woman, you should have fought harder to win."

"But—"

"Move," Ral barked. "Get out of my way *now*!"

The man must have finally stepped out of Ral's way, since they were moving again. She heard soft voices but she didn't push against the man holding her to chance looking up. She was afraid that whatever was around her wasn't something she wanted to see.

The man made several turns before he stopped. His hands left her, but he kept her tucked over his wide shoulder. She heard the sound of rock scraping against rock. Ral moved and turned, and another scraping noise followed. He gripped her again so she wouldn't fall as he bent over slowly.

Ariel's bare feet touched cool stone. The arm around her legs released her and the hand on her ass let go. They both straightened up to face each other. Ariel's chin lifted. She met his eyes briefly before turning her attention to the room around her.

It was a small space, dimly lit. Rough rock walls surrounded them. A thick mattress with blankets sat in one corner and a pile of clothing took up another. She saw a rough door made out of a sheet of rock. It was the only way in or out.

"What are you called?" His voice was deep as he growled the words.

She startled, her eyes flying to meet his. "Ariel."

He blinked, his eyes glowing. She swallowed, locking her gaze with his. A deep breath made his massive chest expand even farther.

"I am Ral. I am Zorn. What are you?"

"Human. I'm from Earth."

"They took you from your home planet as well?"

She nodded. "Days ago. They said they're looking for breeders but I'm not compatible with them."

His attention lowered to her body. "Remove your clothing."

Ariel backed up. Fear hit her hard. "No!"

He frowned. "Now."

She backed up farther, shaking her head. "What do you want?"

"To see if you are compatible with *me*."

Her throat went dry. "No."

He softly growled. "I will not hurt you. I want to look at you to see if we are compatible."

She shook her head again and looked for an escape.

The man moved fast, grabbing her around her waist. She gasped as her feet left the floor. In seconds, the man had her flat on her back on his mattress. It was soft, and it smelled like him. His body straddled her hips as he grabbed her wrists. She fought but he was far too strong.

He pulled her wrists together and easily held them in one huge fist. She stared at his hands, so like hers, only larger. He had roughened skin on his palm and the pads of his fingertips.

He reached for his waist to yank off the rope-like belt holding up his pants. He wound it around her wrists securely before shoving her hands above her head.

"Don't move."

She was petrified. "Please don't hurt me!"

He blinked and frowned at her. "I have no intention of hurting you."

She didn't move her arms. She didn't move *anything*. The man was too strong and big, and Ariel knew she didn't stand a chance to win in a physical fight against him.

His gaze went to her bra as he reached for it. Ariel tensed when the man gripped the material between her breasts. With a tug, her bra ripped apart. He shoved the cups aside so he could stare at her breasts. He softly growled.

"The same."

She fought the urge to struggle. Her heart was pounding and she barely held in a whimper. "What is the same?"

"Your breasts are like those of our women." He scooted down her until he straddled her knees. He visually inspected her underwear and reached for them.

"Don't," Ariel pleaded softly.

He froze. His gaze lifted to meet hers. His intense eyes narrowed slightly. "I want to make sure I won't hurt you."

Ariel *did* whimper when the man gripped her underwear and tore them off. He shifted his body, then gripped her thighs, pushing them apart. He scooted up until he was sitting on his heels with his body between her spread legs. Ral's complete attention went to where her underwear used to be.

He unleashed another soft growl and his gaze met hers. "Explain how you have sex on your world."

Ariel pleaded with him. "Don't do this."

"We *are* doing this. I want you." He reached for the waist of his pants. "I will try to have sex your way but if you won't tell me what I want to know, we'll have sex *my* way."

Her heart was pounding. "I don't know what to say."

He growled. "Have you shared your body with a male before?"

"Yes." Her voice shook.

"How do you and your males have sex?"

"Look, until I was kidnapped, I never even realized people from other planets existed. Please don't do this!"

He tilted his head. "Your world doesn't have space travel?"

"We do, but there's no planet close enough for us to reach where life exists. We've only looked at nearby planets. They didn't hold life."

"Life exists on many other worlds." He spread her thighs wider, his eyes roaming down her body. "Tell me what arouses you. This will happen regardless, so tell me what you need to enjoy it."

She was too afraid.

He growled. "*I want you.* Show me what you like or you might not enjoy what I do to you."

Fighting a sob, Ariel nodded, her eyes traveling down his body. "What do *you* do for sex?"

He opened his pants. Ariel gasped.

She stared at his cock as mild fear hit her. He was very similar to humans only he was a larger, thicker, and the head of his cock was more mushroomed.

"Do I look like your males?"

She swallowed hard. "You're a little bigger."

He touched her, spreading her labia with his fingers, and looked between her folds. With his other hand, he explored her slit. One finger sank into her pussy and Ariel's breath left her. The man had thick fingers.

He pushed into her deeper and growled. "You can take me."

"Please don't do this," she whispered.

He shook his head. "It's happening. I have a strong need. There is no use fighting, so show or tell me what arouses you."

"Release my wrists. Please?" Her voice shook.

He nodded and held out his hand after withdrawing his finger from inside her. She lifted her arms, holding them out, and he unfastened the belt binding her wrists before tossing it away. He growled at her.

"Show me. Touch yourself the way you like to be touch."

She stared up into his eyes. "Please…"

He growled again and bent down until inches separated them. "You have been taken. You are a slave now, just like we are. They won't permit you to go home. You *belong* to me. I will protect you and feed you. I will be the only man who touches you. In exchange, you will let me have you for pleasure." His eyes narrowed. "I won't hurt you. Show me what you like so we both may *share* pleasure—or take your chances of me hurting you when I take my own. Do we understand each other? I am your life now."

She blinked back hot tears and nodded. "I understand."

"Touch yourself and show me how you feel pleasure."

She was shaking as she put her finger in her mouth. She wet it and reached between them, Ral leaning back to get a better view of her. He spread her thighs wider, his focus glued to her sex as she used her other hand to spread herself. Ariel touched her clit with a fingertip and drew slow circles.

Shutting her eyes made the task easier. Ariel had never masturbated in front of someone before. She was embarrassed, having a hard time getting over her fear. Opening her eyes slightly after a moment, she gazed at him. Ral was watching her finger move in tight circles against her clit. He was breathing harder, his chest rising fast and harsh, and a look of hunger masked his features.

He suddenly inserted his finger inside her pussy again. He pushed in another finger just seconds later. He pumped them slowly inside her as she rubbed her clit.

A tingling sensation made her breathe harder. She moaned. He softly growled back.

She was slowly getting turned on as her fear lessened, the feeling of him finger-fucking her while she rubbed her clit exciting. Even his soft growls began to arouse her. She felt almost perverse, enjoying such animalistic sounds, but it was starting to feel too good for her to care.

Ariel rubbed faster on her clit, crying out as her climax hit out of nowhere.

A low moan rumbled from the back of Ral's throat as he slowly withdrew his fingers. "I felt you. You are so tight against my fingers. You are wet now. Wet and ready for me."

He gripped her hips as he moved back and turned her over. She gasped at his effortless strength. Ral spread her thighs and knelt between them, sitting back on his heels. Gripping her hips, he lifted Ariel off the mattress, pulling her back until her spread thighs were straddling his legs. Then he yanked her even higher on his lap, until he was pressing against her wet slit with his cock.

He pushed into her slowly.

Ariel fisted his bedding and whimpered. He was thick and he didn't pause as he continued to slowly enter her body, forcing her to take him. He was so thick it almost hurt. A growl tore from his throat as he pushed deeper.

Ariel soon felt her groin flush against his body, Ral totally buried inside her as he hesitated. The sensation of being stretched by his thick cock was almost overwhelming.

He released her hips and large hands cupped her ass. His rough palms rubbed her skin and he growled.

"So good. So hot and wet. So soft. Lord of the Moons, woman."

She moaned as he withdrew a few inches and pushed into her again. He moved slowly at first and then increased the pace. His hands slid from her ass to wrap around her hips, where he gripped her firmly. Then Ral lifted her hips a few inches above his lap and started to pound in and out of her fast…faster.

The sensations made Ariel moan and pant. Shockingly, he was making her feel more pleasure than she'd ever experienced.

Ral slid one hand around her belly. He cupped her mound and quickly found her clit. Two thick fingers brushed against her sensitive nub with every movement he made. Ariel was soaked, the wetness drenching her thighs. She was overloaded by raw pleasure.

She screamed out as she came hard.

The man behind her roared as his body jerked violently. Ariel felt hot cum jetting inside her in strong bursts. Ral slowed his pace as he moved inside her, until he eventually stopped. They were both out of breath.

"You are mine to keep," he growled softly.

Ariel closed her eyes. She shivered. Being seduced by a sexy yet scary alien was the best sex she'd ever had in her life.

She fought tears. God, her life was so fucked up.

The man eased his cock out slowly as left her body. He collapsed on the bed next to her and pulled her into his arms, making her face him. She opened her eyes to stare at his flushed features. He frowned as he studied her eyes.

"Your eyes are wet."

"Tears."

"What are those?"

She blinked them back. "When humans are sad or hurt, we get tears. Our eyes water and they spill down our faces."

He frowned. "I hurt you? I thought you enjoyed it."

"I did." She wasn't going to lie to him. "I enjoyed it too much. I don't even know you."

He rubbed her hip with his large hand. "This hurts you, that you didn't know me before we bred?"

She nodded. "I've never allowed anyone to touch me before without being in love first."

"Being what?" He looked confused.

She bit her lip for a second. "When you want to spend all your life with one person, because you have so many feelings for them that you don't want to live without them. They are everything to you. That's being in love."

He nodded. "Then do not get tears. We are in love. You are mine. I will never let you go. You will spend your life with me and no one else. I am now everything to you, and you are now everything to me. I will die to protect and keep you safe. I will always care for you."

She was shocked. "I don't think you understand."

He arched a black eyebrow. "I think *you* do not understand. You are mine for life. I won you. I claimed you. I will keep you. We will breed often and I am hoping you will take my seed to root."

"'Seed to root'?"

He touched her stomach. "I hope my seed makes you grow with my offspring."

Shock tore through her again. "You want to get me pregnant?"

"There's no translation for pregnant. It is just the word."

"You want me to have a baby?"

He shrugged. "Offspring."

She nodded. "A baby."

"Yes. I wish you to have one with me. Many with me."

"What if we aren't compatible?"

"It won't make me give you up. You are mine. We take a woman to bound with for life. I have taken you. You are mine whether we have offspring or not."

She stared up at him. He softly growled.

"I want you again. Roll onto your stomach."

He went to his knees again and sat on his bent legs. He patted his thighs. "Up."

She hesitated. "Do you always have sex that way?"

"Yes. You do not?"

"Sometimes. We like different positions."

"But I can't hit your *unis* in any other position."

"*Unis*?"

"The *unis* is what makes you enjoy sex. Without it, you cannot enjoy sex at all."

She eyed him. "I don't think I have a *unis*, and I still enjoyed sex with you."

He suddenly gripped and rolled her to her stomach. "Relax."

She gasped when he pushed two fingers inside her pussy. He was pushing deep, pressing back on her inner walls, toward her spine. He twisted both digits, searching for something. Ariel struggled.

"That hurts!"

He withdrew his fingers and she heard him growl. Ariel turned her head to stare up at him. A confused look had taken over his rugged features.

"You don't have one."

"What is it?"

"It is a hard, round, finger-shaped nerve bundle that I must rub during sex."

She rolled over onto her back and spread her thighs, so she knew he had a good view of her. His gaze lowered. "See this?" She touched her clit. "I think that's where my *unis* is. The other side of this inside of me, it's another pleasure spot. When you stroke me in those places, it makes me come."

Desire was evident on his features. He reached down to finger her clit. Ariel moaned. Ral growled low in response. Ariel lifted her hips and scooted closer to him. She eased her ass onto his lap.

"Take me this way while you touch me."

She saw shock but also interest on his expressive face. He gripped his hard shaft, rubbing it against her slit. She was really wet. He groaned as he pushed into her all the way. His finger played with her clit as he started to rock his hips.

"Lord of the Moons," he groaned. "This feels good."

Ariel planted her feet on the mattress and moved her hips to meet his thrusts. She gripped the sides of his calves to get leverage, to move faster on him. She knew she wasn't going to last long. The man wasn't letting up on her clit as he drove into her fast and deep. She tensed and felt her body clamping down on his cock.

Ariel screamed out as she came hard.

Her eyes flew open. She stared up at Ral, watching as he threw his head back. His features tensed. His mouth opened. She saw sharp teeth revealed between his parted lips as he groaned deep in his throat, just before his cock pulsed strongly inside her. His semen shot deep into her when he came.

They were both panting. Ral's eyes opened as he dropped his head, staring at Ariel. A grin spread his mouth. "You are amazing."

"So are you."

Chapter Three

"Wake."

Ariel opened her eyes and turned her head. She was sleeping on her stomach. Ral was sitting up. She stared at him and he smiled back at her.

"It is time to eat and go to work. You must come with me." He reached over to brush her blonde hair from her cheek. His fingers wrapped around one of the natural curls, then moved to trail down the length of her neck, before he pulled away. "It is time to work."

She nodded. "What do we do for work?"

He stood up, stretching his naked body. Ariel swallowed. The man was beautiful and his muscular body was perfection. He walked forward, leaned down, and Ariel continued to appreciate the view of his tan, muscular ass. He withdrew some clothes and turned to face the bed.

"You will just stay close to me. You can fetch me water when I need it."

She nodded. "Okay." She crawled from the bed.

Ral handed her clothing from his pile. The shirt and pants were huge. She studied them with raised eyebrows and Ral laughed.

"I will get you smaller clothing soon. This is what I have."

She put them on. The pants were several sizes too large and fell down her hips. Ral went to his knees in front of her, still naked, and used the rope-like belt he'd used on her wrists to secure the pants at her waist. His shirt almost went to her knees. She suddenly wished he hadn't destroyed her bra and underwear.

"I need to go to the bathroom."

"Bathroom?"

She flushed a little. "I have to pee. I have liquid inside I must release."

He grinned. "Urinate."

"Yes."

He nodded. "We will urinate before breakfast."

"Okay."

He rose to his feet to put on some pants, but she noted he didn't have shoes. He bent and picked up what looked like a hairbrush, tackling his long hair before walking behind her. His hands were gentle as he brushed her hair as well. He threw the brush down on the clothes pile and walked to the door, pushing it open. Ral offered his hand when he turned to face her. She moved toward him and put her smaller hand in his larger one.

"Come."

The hallway was dimly lit and empty of other people. He led her down a corridor then turned. An open archway took them into a large room, where she saw a crude bathroom of sorts, with open shower stalls, some weird-looking toilets and three waterfall-like holes in the wall. She walked over to one of the toilets to study it. They almost looked like urinals.

He chuckled. "Not like your world?"

She shook her head. "No."

He grinned, but it disappeared when he said, "I will guard the door. Never permit another man to see your bare skin." His bright eyes narrowed. "They will want to breed with you and I will kill them. If another tries to touch you, yell for me. You never go from my sight."

She nodded. "I don't want anyone touching me but you, or seeing me without my clothing."

His large body relaxed. "Go. I will guard the door to not let anyone in."

She used the bathroom quickly and retied her belt. "Ral? I'm done."

He came back into the room and walked to a mini waterfall. He unfastened his pants as she watched and turned his head to grin at her as he used the wall. He looked amused that she was so curious. He fastened his pants and walked toward her, taking her hand and leading her to a washbowl, so both of them could clean their hands.

He led her down corridors that twisted and turned. She smelled something good that made her stomach growl loudly. Ral turned his head to eye her.

"You hunger greatly?"

She nodded. "I haven't eaten in a long time. I'm starving."

"They have not fed you since taking you from your planet?"

"They gave me food once when they first grabbed me. It's been days."

Rage hardened his face. "I *hate* them."

She understood hating the Anzons too. They walked into a large room. Tables had been set up and she saw about fifty men, but only two women. She couldn't help but stare at the females. Their features revealed them as

Zorn; she could tell by their wide, flat noses. They had breasts and smaller facial features than the men, and they were attractive. The women eyed her back. Ariel gave them a smile but both Zorn women looked away from her.

Ariel sighed. It didn't look like she would be making friends.

A buffet-style table had been laid out. A Zorn man was serving. He stared openly at Ariel. Her hand tightened on Ral's, and he smiled at her.

"They are curious. We have never seen a homin before."

"Human."

He chuckled. "*Human.*"

She smiled up at him. "Right."

"From the planet Earth."

"Yes. You remembered."

He stopped at the table, studying it. "Do you recognize anything you can eat?"

She studied the food too and shook her head. "No."

"This," he pointed, "is very sweet. This is bitter. This is strongly hot to your mouth." He kept pointing out things to her and explaining their taste. She settled on a few things to try then Ral loaded down two plates and walked to a table where no one else sat.

"Sit. I will get us drinks."

She sat down with both plates and Ral returned in moments, placing water-filled mugs by their plates. He smiled. "Eat, Ariel."

She loved the way he said her name. It sounded like "Ori-All".

She tasted the food and gave Ral a smile. It was delicious. He looked relieved as he dug into his own, occasionally picking up something from his plate for her to taste. She decided she didn't like the red banana-looking thing. It set her mouth on fire and made her choke. She gulped water to try to kill the heat.

When they finished their food, Ral led her to a wide hallway. "Stay with me. Do not leave my side. It is dangerous."

Ariel nodded and felt a little fear. "What's dangerous?"

"My people were taken by force from our hunt planet. We are strong and we are good fighters. Do you understand? There were few women taken with us. A woman is rare and much wanted here. Some will be angry that they lost yesterday, when we fought for you. They will want to touch you. If a fight breaks out, just get behind me. I will not lose. I am very hardy. I will win."

She nodded. He reached up to caress her cheek.

"Some Zorn will think I only won so I may mount you, to quench my need for a woman. They might think I won't shed their blood for an alien. In time they will realize I am bound to you, and will not dare challenge me for your body."

"Bound to you?"

He grinned. "It is like love."

She smiled shyly. "Okay."

"They will offer me things to have you. I will not sell you for anything, so do not worry if you hear them make offers. You are mine. You will remain mine."

Ariel put her hand on his naked chest. The men didn't seem to wear shirts but she didn't know why. He obviously owned them, since she wore his. "I trust you."

He smiled. "Good. We should go. Stay close to me."

The mines were a large cavern area where men were chipping away at the rock-lined walls to enlarge the space. Some men hung by their waists from harnesses, using tools to carve into the stone to break larger pieces loose and reach high into the cavern. Ral sat Ariel on a large boulder, gave her a nod, and then went to work. He picked up the broken pieces from the floor to load them into machines that wheeled away from sight when Ral pushed a button after each cart became full. An empty one would instantly appear in its place.

After a short while, Ariel got up to stand closer to Ral. She picked up the smaller pieces and started to work with him. Ral looked over at her with a surprised expression but she just smiled back.

They worked together for hours. She noticed three Zorn women in the cavern, who all sat by their men but didn't help. She caught many eyes watching her.

A buzz went through the room. Ral dumped a basketball-sized rock in the car before turning to Ariel. "We are done. Our shift is over. Thank you for helping me."

"I can't lift the big ones like you do but I'm good with the small chunks."

He laughed. "Hungry?"

"Yes. Very much."

He led her back to the large eating room. It was packed now. Ral gripped her arm, pulling her tightly against his side, and she knew instantly there was potential danger with a larger crowd. She could feel it in the alert way Ral watched every man around them.

They moved up the line to the buffet table. Ral filled plates for both of them, handed them to Ariel, and got water with her by his side this time. He led them to a crowded table, put down the waters and sat. He gestured to his thighs.

"Sit on my lap."

She eased onto his lap after placing the food down. He scooted back and spread his thighs, so she had room between them to sit on the bench.

A man sitting next to them sniffed loudly and turned his head. Ariel met a pair of bright green eyes. The man sniffed again and growled. Ariel dropped her gaze from his. She could feel Ral tense as he snarled.

"Mine."

The man next to them inched away about a foot. Ral leaned into Ariel until his lips pressed to her ear and he said something in soft growls. She frowned before she realized he was talking in her wrong ear. She turned her head so she could look up at him and pointed to her other ear.

"This is the only one they implanted. I didn't understand a thing you said."

He frowned. "Only one of your ears is implanted?"

She nodded.

"I said don't meet anyone's eyes and eat fast."

She nodded and turned to face her food, eating quickly. Ral wolfed his down. He rubbed her arm then lowered his face again to her ear, the right one this time, to whisper to her.

"Ready to leave?"

"Yes."

"We'll go to the urinate room and then go back to our room."

"Sounds good."

Ral helped Ariel to her feet then stood, pulling her against his side. They headed toward the door.

They were almost out of the room when three men moved to stand in their way. Ral tensed, easing Ariel behind him. He growled at the three men.

"Move."

One of the men frowned. "Share her. We have needs, and she is a different species. She's not a Zorn woman."

"She's *mine*. I have bound her," Ral growled. "Move away from my woman or I will kill you to protect her."

Ariel turned her head. Some more men had stepped closer. They stared openly at her body. She didn't like the hungry looks on their faces. She inched closer to Ral, trying to mold herself to his back as fear crept in.

He turned his head and snarled. The men moved back but not far enough away for Ariel's comfort. Ral faced the three men in front of them once more.

"Gru, if you do this, you will die. Do you understand me? I have given to our people plenty. I will keep her. I will kill anyone who tries to take her from me. She is not to share. She is bound to me." He eyed the men with Gru. "I will kill you all if you don't back away now."

"Then one of us will die—but we want her," Gru snarled.

Ral snarled back. He turned his head. "Rham, Ler, Hosh, protect her."

Three large men moved forward, shoving others out of their way. Ral looked at Ariel. "My pack. They will protect you. Go with them."

Terror hit her hard. "Ral—"

"You will be in my sight. They will make sure you stay there."

The three large men surrounded Ariel. One of them gripped her arm and yanked her against the wall, out of the way. She stared at the men protecting her, wondering what a "pack" meant to Zorn, but she had no time to think about it. She heard a roar and jerked her head toward Ral.

Four men attacked him instead of three.

Horror filled Ariel. She looked up at one of the three big men. "Can't you help him fight?"

One of the men shook his head. "You are Ral's woman to fight for. We only guard you. It is our way."

"Your way sucks," she whispered. Terror for Ral hit her as she watched him fight.

Ral was damn good. There were four men surrounding him. Two of them grabbed his arms while the third man gripped him from behind. The fourth came at him from the front. It was Gru.

42

Ariel gasped and tried to run to Ral. She wanted to jump on one of those bastards. Ral needed help!

One of the men ordered to protect her gripped her arm, yanking her back.

"Stay," he said softly. "Ral needs no help."

Ral threw his head back, slamming his skull into the face of the man behind him. Both of Ral's feet shot out in the same instant to kick Gru. Both men gripping Ral's arms staggered backward, trying to keep hold of him. He knocked both of them off balance with his powerful kick to Gru's chest.

Gru roared in pain. His body flew backward, slamming hard into a rough rock wall.

When Ral's feet hit the floor, he yanked his arms together. It sent the men holding him arms crashing into each other. Ral jerked an arm free from one of the men to slam his fist into the face closest to him.

It was brutal. It was bloody. Ral beat the hell out of all four of them. The men on the floor were bleeding profusely and some of them had broken bones. Ariel learned that Zorn also fought with their teeth. Ral had torn up one man's arm when the man had tried to batter Ral's face.

When the four men were down, Ral turned to snarl at the room. He walked over and grabbed Gru by his hair, yanking the man up to his unsteady feet.

"She is *mine*. I told you it would cost you your life, Gru." Ral glared around the room. "Death to *any* man who tries to touch the woman I bound to."

Ariel almost collapsed when she watched Ral snap Gru's neck. He just twisted it effortlessly and she heard the popping sound.

He threw Gru's body down. He grabbed up the next man, who whimpered.

"Please, Ral—"

Ral broke his neck as well before throwing him aside.

Ariel closed her eyes, fighting a sob. She heard two more pops. Both of the remaining men had begged for their lives. Ral hadn't hesitated to kill them.

"She's mine!" he roared.

Ariel's eyes flew open when a hand gripped her.

A bloody Ral was panting as he jerked on her hand. She stumbled after him when he didn't give her a choice, dragging her from the room, around the dead bodies of the men he'd fought, and down the corridor. He didn't stop until he reached the bathroom. He yanked her inside. Two men occupied the room. Ral snarled at them both.

"Out. Baras, guard the door."

One of the men nodded, glancing at Ariel. "Are you all right, Ral?"

"I had to kill four men stupid enough to try to take my bound woman."

The man paled. "I will guard the door."

"Appreciated," Ral said, quieter now.

He stared down at Ariel. She looked up at him with fear. He frowned. "Why are you looking at me like that?"

"You killed all four of them."

He softly growled at her. "I don't know how things are on your planet, but you aren't there anymore, Ariel. If I did not kill them, then I would have to fight to keep you every day. Would you prefer I let them take you? Do you know what they would have done with you? They would have bred you until they were sated and then passed you to other men. You are little. You would not survive long. They would hurt you. You are mine. You and I are in love. Do you understand?"

She nodded. "I've just…" She fought tears. "It scared me and I'm not used to violence. I realize you had no choice and I appreciate that you did that for me. I really do. I'm just in shock."

He sighed as his hold on her arm loosened. "I will wash. Remove your clothes. We wash together."

She stripped quickly. She kept glancing at the door but Ral shook his head. "Baras won't let anyone enter. Most of my people fear me. I am stronger than all."

"You fight really well."

"I am a…" He hesitated. "I don't know how to make you understand. On my planet, some are stronger than others. I am from the strongest family. My father leads our planet."

She was stunned. "Like a king?"

"I don't know that word. My father is the strongest. He leads all of our people."

"Shit. You're like a prince."

He shrugged. "I don't understand that term but my people follow me here. Sometimes some of them get stupid. They forget I fight the best. It is

45

our way. The strongest lead the weaker. I am the strongest of my people here."

"So why did they even fight you in that arena?"

"To win you from the Anzons." He hesitated. "We do not like to injure each other but we are good at inflicting enough injury to make it look real. Sometimes we pretend broken bones. Sometimes the fight is real. Some fought for real for you. I always win the fight, and award the prize to one of my people who deserve it. This time, I kept the prize for myself."

She was shocked again by the man who jerked her naked body into the shower stall and waved his hand against the wall. A waterfall of warm water fell from above the entire shower stall area like rain. It startled Ariel.

Ral chuckled. "The water cleans us. It will clean all. Just rub it on your skin."

"There's nothing to wash our hair with?"

He held out a hand, letting the rain collect and fall. "It cleans your hair. There are chemicals in the water. Do not swallow it. It won't harm you or your eyes, I do not think, since it gets in our eyes as well, but it doesn't taste good. If you swallow much it will come back up."

"So that whole fight to win me from the Anzons wasn't real?"

He hesitated. "We learned long ago when we were first captured how to show a fight to make it look good or they would withhold food to all, to make us fight for real. Some fight for real to try to win prizes they desire with much greed. Many fought for real for you. They were being foolish; they wanted to win you so they could share you. They knew they were not in favor with me, and I would not find them deserving of you if I were to give away my prize, so they fought."

"Was Gru the man who stopped you yesterday, to ask who I was being given to?"

He nodded. "Gru did not like that I kept you; he thought he was deserving enough that I would award you to him. But I have more than earned the right to withhold you for myself."

"You've won other women?"

"Yes."

Jealousy hit her. "You bred with them?"

He watched her with narrowed lids. "No. I have always handed them over immediately to those men I deemed deserving." He reached to cup her face gently with his hand. He brushed his thumb along her cheek. "You are the only woman I have taken to my bed since we were stolen from our planet. That was six months ago."

She was shocked again. "Why did you keep me? Why didn't you keep any of those other women?"

He smiled. "I was attracted to you so strongly, I felt it in my blood when I laid eyes upon you. I had to have you."

She nodded. "I'm glad."

"I am glad as well. Let's go to our room. I feel the need for you in my blood—and I don't think it would be safe for me to have you here."

Chapter Four

Ral shut the door firmly. "Remove your clothes."

She stripped quickly, watching as Ral remove his pants, already fully aroused. He walked to the mattress, kneeled down, then sat back on his legs. He tapped his lap.

"Up or down. Your choice."

Ariel smiled. "Do you always sit on your legs?"

"Your kind does not?"

"No. Stretch out flat on your back for me."

He hesitated but then did as she'd asked. She dropped to her knees and climbed on the mattress, massaging his chest as she straddled his lap. Desire burned in his eyes as he watched her silently but he didn't protest. She leaned over him, lightly licking his chest, and instantly his body tensed. Growling, he arched his back to bring his body closer to her mouth.

She took that for a good sign. Next she licked his nipple and sucked it into her mouth.

He slid his hands into her hair with a groan. "Lord of the Moons," he whispered.

Ariel smiled as she released his nipple. "Who is this guy?"

Ral chuckled. "The protector and watcher of my planet."

"God."

"Is that who protects your planet and watches over it?"

She hesitated. "Is your Lord of the Moons a breathing person or someone you believe in?"

"A belief."

She nodded. "I have God."

"Do that again with your mouth."

She lowered her face to play with his nipple in her lips and tongue. She brushed kisses across his chest to tease the other nipple, before drawing back slightly to blow air on his wet skin. She grinned as his nipple puckered.

Ral groaned. "I need you."

She gripped his thick erection in her hand, already turned on and wet. She stared into his eyes as she adjusted him under her hips, moaning when she slid down, taking him into her body. He felt damn good. She lowered herself until he was buried deep inside her. Ral growled low.

"Ariel, that feels so amazing."

"Wait." She moved on him, riding him slowly.

Ral gripped her hips, tossing back his head. He thrust upward into her as she drove down. They moved faster and faster together as the pleasure grew.

"Touch me," she gasped. "I'm so close."

He released one of her hips so his hand was free to touch her clit. He rubbed it between his finger and thumb, fast and hard. That was all it took. Ariel screamed out and came, Ral snarling as his hot body jerked. He pulsed deep inside her and threw back his head as he came.

Ariel collapsed on his chest, smiling against his skin. "So...was that as good as when you sit on your legs?"

"Better," he breathed.

"Your women don't enjoy sex unless it's just that one way?"

He rubbed her ass with his hands. "Their *unis* can only be rubbed by the *hais* of our staffs while in that position."

"*Hais*?"

He rolled them over so Ariel was pinned under his larger body. He withdrew from her slowly and went to his knees. Ral gripped his cock, touching the top ridge of it. "*Hais*. Feel. It is rougher than the underside."

She explored the tip of his cock. Ral had a bumped area at the top of his mushroom-shaped head. It was hard and ridged. She saw him shiver as she rubbed her fingertips over that spot. He closed his eyes with a groan.

"Sensitive area?"

"Very."

She slid her fingers to the underside. "What about here?"

"It feels good but the *hais* is the most sensitive."

"When you're inside me, that spot is rubbed no matter what position you're in?" She released him and moved back.

Ral nodded. "When Zorn men punish a woman, some of them will breed her in a position that will keep her from pleasure."

"I don't understand."

He grinned. "We are a male-dominant society."

"I still don't understand."

He lay back down and pulled her into his arms so they were curled together. "If a woman is too willful and needs a reminder that her man is in charge, he will breed her without giving her pleasure, until she submits to him."

"You'd hurt a woman?"

"No. Imagine me arousing you but refused to let you orgasm."

"That's mean."

He laughed. "It is a lesson. When a woman submits, then we make her come."

She rubbed his chest with her fingertips. Ariel loved touching Ral. "That won't work with me."

"I would find a way around it. What would happen if I didn't rub your *unis* in front?"

"I'd still enjoy it. Just not as much."

"How else do you enjoy being bred?"

"Do you have oral sex?"

He got a confused look.

She grinned. "Using your mouth on my *unis*—or me using my mouth on your *hais*."

The confused look disappeared. He nodded. "Women can but unless a man has a very long tongue, we can't reach a *unis* with our mouths. They are about six inches inside a woman."

"That sucks for your women."

"They enjoy finger stimulation." His hand ran down her body. He stopped at her hip. "Your *unis* is very accessible."

She nodded.

He lifted her, pinning Ariel on her back, and smiled down at her. "Let's see how this works."

She hesitated. "I should take a shower first."

He chuckled. "Because I'll taste myself on you? I don't mind." He moved down her and gripped her thighs. "I want to experiment on you."

She spread her thighs wide. "Anything you want."

Ral moved between her thighs, studying her body closely. He lowered his head to stare between her legs. Fingers parted her to give him a perfect view of her clit.

"So pretty."

Ariel laughed. "You think I'm pretty down there?"

He inhaled. "You smell really good too." His mouth lowered and his tongue touched her clit, then he sucked on her. Ariel moaned.

His mouth instantly released her. "Good?"

"Yes!"

"You taste delicious. I will do to you what *I* like, to see if you like it."

"I can't wait," she said breathlessly.

Ral licked and sucked, first slow then fast, using his teeth to lightly scrape against her clit. Ariel moaned louder and clawed the bed. "Ral, that feels so good..."

He growled, vibrating against her. His mouth was merciless as he continued to play, bringing her intense pleasure. It didn't take long at all for Ariel to cry out his name when she came again.

Ral lifted his head from between her spread thighs. "I want to do this often."

"I'll let you." She lifted her head, grinning at him. "Your turn. Roll over onto your back."

He smiled back as he sprawled flat for her. Ariel rose up and climbed between his spread thighs, staring at his impressive erection.

"Tell me what you like, Ral."

"Show me how *your* men like this."

She licked her lips, gripped him tightly in her fist, then ran her tongue over the top of his cock.

He groaned softly, fisting the blankets. His muscles tensed all over his body. "Good," he growled.

She ran her tongue down the underside of his shaft and licked upward, then wrapped her lips around his cock and sucked him into her mouth. Groaning loudly, now Ral clawed at the bedding.

"Lord of the Moons! That feels so good..."

She moved her mouth on him slowly, taking him deeper. Ral's body bucked a little under Ariel as she moved faster, sucking on him harder, using her tongue to tease him unmercifully. Ral's huge body shook seconds before he came in her mouth.

Ariel swallowed without thought—and she was in for a shock.

Ral's semen was warmer than anything she'd ever experienced and he tasted as sweet as candy.

She moaned and kept milking him until every drop was gone then licked him clean.

Ral took a shaky breath. "You are killing me."

She released him from her mouth and the dazed look on his face made her laugh. "You liked that?"

He yanked her on top of him. "I like your way better. Lord of the Moons, was that amazing."

"What was different?"

"Our women only lick the top. They don't take us into their mouths like that. Your way is…" He shivered. "So much better."

She cuddled into Ral. "We have great sex together."

He laughed. "We do. I am ready for sleep. Are you ready for sleep? We did not rest enough last sleep cycle."

"Ummm. Someone wore me out."

Snuggling closer to Ral's large body, Ariel closed her eyes, feeling happily sated wrapped in his arms.

Both of them were starting to drift off to sleep when someone pounded on the door.

Ral growled as he moved Ariel. He grabbed the blankets and covered her body completely from neck to toes. "Stay," he ordered her. He jumped from the bed, grabbing his pants and yanking them on.

Ariel clutched the blanket over her body, feeling a moment of fear. Were more men going to be at the door wanting to fight Ral for her?

Ral shoved the door open and glared at whoever was there. Ariel couldn't see around his large body blocking her view. She heard a soft male voice though she couldn't make out the words.

"I will be there in minutes." He shut the door. "Dress, Ariel. We must go fast."

She was alarmed, but she moved. She climbed out of bed to dress quickly. Ral helped her with her belt. She looked up at him. "What is wrong?"

"We have a meeting to go to. It is very important. One of my pack heard something they need to share."

"What does pack mean? I don't understand the term."

"It means loyal to me and my family. They are trustworthy and won't turn on me. They have earned my trust and that of my family. It is a deep friendship bond. Do you understand?"

"Yes."

Ral gripped her face and studied her. "Do you in love with me, Ariel?"

She stared up at him. She knew what he was asking her even if his words weren't exactly right. He wanted to know if she had feelings for him.

She nodded. She did. She wasn't sure how it had happened in a day…maybe because he was kind, especially compared to the Anzons; maybe because he made her feel safe in this strange, foreign new life thrust upon her…but she *did* love Ral. He'd killed to protect and keep her. He made her laugh. He made love to her. How could she not love him?

"I love you."

"Can I trust you?"

She nodded, never looking away from his eyes. "Yes."

"I have no doubt but I had to ask. Let's go. This is very important."

He pushed open the door and grabbed her hand, walking so fast that Ariel had to run to keep up with him or risk being dragged along. They ended up in someone's sleep room very similar to the one she shared with Ral. The room was crammed with men. Ral pulled Ariel in front of him, his arms locked around her possessively. The door was sealed behind them.

"What has been heard that might help us?" Ral's voice was low.

A man stood up. He nodded at Ral and then his eyes flashed to Ariel. "We can trust her?"

"She is bound to me," Ral growled. He sounded angry. "Do not insult my woman."

The man paled. "I meant no insult to your woman." The man lowered his eyes.

"Speak," Ral sighed.

The man nodded, looking up again, meeting Ral's gaze. "They are preparing one of the large ships. There is a planet they are going to invade for more workforces. Their plan is to house them inside the ship, until we can dig out more area for them to reside here with us."

Ral grinned. "When?"

The man grinned back. "They leave tomorrow morning right at first shift. It is perfect. The plan we overheard was that they will bring back a few hundred workers they are plotting to steal."

Ral's grin faded. He glanced at the men around him. "Our time has come. This is it. Make all the arrangements and do it very quietly. Do not tell the others what is to happen. We will surprise all. You all know what to do. We will wake two hours earlier than first shift to prepare." His gaze swung to the man who had spoken before. "Is everything in place?"

"Yes."

Ral's expression became almost mirthful. "We are so close."

The men were all nodding, eyes flashing.

Ariel took in each one of them. Why they were so excited about new prisoners was beyond her. Maybe they hoped that most of the prisoners would be women. Maybe they were just lonely and wanted new faces, or more help with the digging. She held her silence until Ral returned them to their room and had firmly shut the door.

"Undress." Sexual hunger shone in his eyes.

She stripped, Ral swiftly grabbing and lifting her up his body. Their eyes locked. They were almost nose to nose.

"If I take you facing me while I'm standing, will you enjoy it?"

"Definitely."

He growled softly at her. Ariel locked her legs around his hips and wrapped her arms around his neck and Ral entered her in a heartbeat. Ariel loved the feel of him stretching her, the position taking him deep. He gripped her ass without pause and slammed her up and down on his cock, almost frenzied.

Ariel buried her face against his shoulder, moaning loudly. She wasn't sure what brought on Ral's wild streak but she was enjoying the hell out of it. She threw her head back and groaned loudly.

"Lord of the Moons," she whispered after she came and Ral had found his release with her.

Ral chuckled. "Exactly. Lord of the Moons, was that good."

He eased out of her body and lowered her to the floor, kissing her before stepping away. "We need sleep."

Ariel nodded and climbed into bed. She held up the blankets for Ral. "Climb on in."

He smiled and lay beside her, pulling her into his body until Ariel's face rested on his chest. "I in love you, Ariel."

She chuckled at his wording. "I'm in love with you too, Ral."

"I'm in love with you. Better?" He rubbed her back with his fingers.

"Perfect," she said honestly. Ral was in love with her.

Chapter Five

"Wake."

Ariel opened her eyes. "Damn, you get up early. Did we sleep long? How do you know what time it is?"

"I hear. We have patrols in the hallway who call out the time. My hearing is keen. Get dressed fast. We must hurry. We have much to do, Ariel."

As she got dressed, she realized Ral did something he hadn't done before. "You're wearing a shirt today?"

"Where we are going today, it is colder than down in the cavern mines."

"Okay."

Ral grabbed the blanket from the bed and Ariel watched him dump all of his clothes piled on the floor into the blanket. Something was definitely up but he wasn't telling her what was going on. He hefted the bag of clothes over his shoulder and shoved open the door before reaching for her hand.

"You stay by me. No matter what, you stay with me, Ariel. You are bound to me. I am bound to you. We belong together."

"I remember. I'm not to leave your sight and I'll stay close to you at all times."

"Very correct."

He took her to the bathroom, where four men were ordered by Ral to leave so she could have privacy. When she was done, he walked in and used the bathroom. Three different men walked in moments later and Ral pulled her closer to his body, jerking his head at her in a clear "don't look" gesture. She shot him an eye roll, but kept her attention on Ral. She hardly wanted to watch three men piss. She'd give *Ral* privacy as well, if she thought he'd let her out of his sight.

They both washed up before leaving the bathroom and like the morning before, Ral took her to the eating room.

"Eat fast." He handed the plates he'd filled with food to Ariel, getting them mugs of water. She eyed the room. It was packed, unlike the morning before, but the room was unusually quiet. Ral sat on the bench at the end of a table, spreading his thighs wide. He inched back, making room for her to sit.

Without him needing to tell her, Ariel slid onto his lap between his thighs. Ral gave slight nods to various men around the room. His people were tense; she could feel it in the air. She wondered what was going on, but when she glanced up at him, he just smiled.

"Ral?"

"Trust me and ask later."

She nodded. They finished eating quickly and then Ral was on the move, Ariel following him out of the eating area. He didn't head toward the mine, though. He gripped the blanket over his shoulder, took her hand and headed in the direction of doors marked in some language she couldn't read. The words simply looked like squiggles and scratches.

The hand holding hers tightened and Ral paused to look down at her.

"Stay with me. If something goes wrong, we will have to run. Swear you will run with me, Ariel. I don't want to lose you. I will die if they take you from me because I will fight them, regardless of the odds."

Fear hit her. What was going on?

Ral opened up the door, which led into a smaller hallway. He jerked her forward and they nearly jogged down the hall that ended at one of those platform-elevator things with the raw rock walls. Ral stepped onto it, pulling her into his arms.

"Do not touch the walls."

"I won't." She shivered. "It would be like brushing up against an electric cheese grater, at the speed these things move up and down," she mumbled.

"Cheese grater?"

"Never mind. I was talking to myself."

The platform slowed and Ral sniffed the air before pulling her forward. They ran down hall after hall until they came to another large door. It looked like the huge, heavy door she'd walked through when Yoz had taken her to the fighting arena. The door swished open.

Ariel was more than a little surprised to see one of Ral's men standing there.

"We are ready. The rest follow."

Ral nodded as he took off running without warning.

His hand on Ariel's hand tightened as he yanked her behind him, making her sprint for all she was worth across the large room to another huge door.

Ral paused, turning his head to look back.

Ariel looked over her shoulder to see dozens of Zorn running into the large room, with more on their heels. The entire room was swiftly filling with Zorn.

When the man who'd let them into the room finally shut the other door, there had to be well over a hundred Zorn in the room, along with a few other species she didn't know and hadn't seen before. Ariel noted the non-Zorn looked as confused as she felt. There were only a handful, all of them females.

"Let's do this." Ral nodded.

The huge door opened and Ariel spun around—a gasp escaping her lips as she saw a massive ship parked in what appeared to be open space. It was only upon looking closer that she saw the glass dome, barely noticeable with deep space as a background.

More Zorn men were already by the ship. They waved frantically at everyone, and like a frenzied stampede, all the Zorn started to run.

Ral pulled her closer to his body and they both ran for the large ship.

Still confused, trying not to be trampled in the chaotic flow of bodies, it wasn't until Ral tried to coax even more speed out of Ariel that comprehension dawned.

They were trying to escape!

Shock tore through her as they ran up a ramp and into the belly of the ship. It looked like a huge cargo area, easily spacious enough to accommodate the large fleeing group. More of Zorn already awaited them inside.

Ral kept running, pulling Ariel with him as they exited the cargo area into a wide metal corridor.

"This way, Argis Ral," a man yelled. "We are getting ready for flight."

Ral wasn't even out of breath as he asked the other man, "Have you damaged the other ships?"

"Yes," the Zorn jogging beside them growled. "They won't be able to follow us. Not for a long time."

Panting hard, a pain shooting through her side, Ariel began to slow her steps. Ral swiftly halted and spun, shoved the wrapped blanket of his clothes at the other man, then in an instant, Ariel was gripped around her middle and slung over Ral's hard shoulder. He started to run again, holding her tight against his body.

They ended up in what she assumed was a ship elevator, Ral holding her securely as slight pressure indicated they were jetting upward. Ariel pushed hair out of her face to stare at the Zorn man standing a few feet from her and Ral.

"The ship is full." The Zorn touched his ear, where a metal device was clipped. "They are securing the cargo doors. We're ready. All are accounted for."

"Let's get out of here," Ral snarled. "Do not wait for me to reach the command center."

"Lift off," the Zorn said. "Argis Ral has ordered liftoff!"

The engines weren't loud but Ariel still heard them as they vibrated to life. The elevator door opened when it stopped and Ral moved quickly into the room beyond. He bent to deposit Ariel on her feet gently before gripping her arm and turning her around.

Ariel stared, wide-eyed in astonishment, at the large window.

The room was like some kind of huge cockpit, with five Zorn working various control stations. Ral moved to the largest seat, tugging Ariel with him. He sat down, pulled her across his lap, and wrapped an arm securely around her waist.

"Report," Ral ordered.

"They triggered the alarm when the ship was started but we've overridden their systems," a man behind them stated. "The dome is retracting. Forty seconds to liftoff."

Ral growled. "Get us out of here now."

"We can only go so fast. They cannot reach the ship. The pressure seals were automatically locked when the dome started to open. They would be sucked out of the dock into space, even if they *could* bypass their own safety measures."

Ral nodded. "What about their defenses?"

"They are destroyed." The man sitting in a chair to their right laughed. "We blew them when you gave the order to lift off. Those blue bastards are busy right now dealing with the fires we set. We will be clear. They cannot stop us."

Ral nodded. Ariel's eyes flew to his but he didn't glance at her, instead he looked grim as he gazed at the large window. "Until we are free and clear, I will not feel too confident, Avi. Viz, have you accessed their charts? Do we know where we are and how to get home?"

"Yes, Argis Ral. We are three weeks from home at full capacity."

Ral closed his eyes and smiled slightly. "Home." His eyes snapped open. "Time?"

"Ten seconds. We are ready. I will alert our people to secure themselves."

Ral tucked Ariel closer to his body. "Hold on, Ariel. This ship has strong engines and we are not easing out. We want to cause damage when we leave here. It will burn up their docking bay."

She wrapped her arms around his neck just as the engines of the ship vibrated harder and the huge ship shot forward.

Ariel's body slammed tightly to Ral's but she managed to turn her head to look at the view, awestruck, as the ship flew into space.

"They have a weapon that didn't blow," a man snarled. "Initiating evasive maneuvers."

Ral growled. "Can we avoid being hit?"

The man laughed. "Not a problem. We are out of range in three, two, one—now. We're free!"

Ral laughed long and hard. He held Ariel in his arms as he stood, his smile wide. "We are free, my Ariel!"

She stared at Ral, too shocked still to speak, and he winked at her. "Open full ship communications." He gently sat Ariel in the seat he'd vacated.

Ariel was still reeling, her thoughts jumbled.

They'd escaped the Anzons.

She hadn't known they were even trying to escape. Ral hadn't told her. She realized now that this was what the meeting had been about the night before. The Zorn hadn't been excited about new prisoners—they had been excited about a large ship being prepared so they could use it to escape.

Hurt came next. Why hadn't Ral told her? Hadn't he trusted her? He'd been keyed up after the meeting, excited enough to fuck her...but he hadn't trusted her with their plan.

Because he wasn't taking her back to Earth...?

Because he *was*...?

Ariel was shocked further to realize she didn't know which she'd prefer herself.

"This is Argis Ral," Ral said loudly. "We are free. In three weeks, we will be returned to our home. We will see Zorn again!"

The men in the room threw back their heads and howled loudly. Ariel startled. Ral smiled widely at her before gazing at the man to his left and running a hand over his throat.

The Zorn nodded. "Communications are off, Argis Ral."

Ral glanced at one of the other men. "Any pursuit?"

"No, Argis Ral. We damaged them too well."

Ral nodded. "Keep a sharp eye out. I don't want any surprises."

"Yes, Argis Ral."

Ral stared out the wide window, his arms crossed over his muscled chest, satisfaction clear on his face.

Ariel swallowed. "Ral?"

He smiled at her. "Yes?"

"Are you taking me home?"

He nodded and moved closer to crouch down in front of her. His hands gripped her face gently. "We are bound. You will be very welcome on my planet."

"I meant Earth," she whispered.

Ral's smile died. "We are bound, Ariel. I must see my people home safely, and I do not know your planet's location. I am sorry. My home is now your home."

She nodded, feeling a little numb, the implications of his words sinking in.

Ral released her and walked to one of the stations. He spoke softly to his men.

Ariel remained in the chair, staring at the velvety blackness of deep space.

He was taking her to his planet. She wasn't ever going to see Earth again.

Pain and anger filled her. His men had access to the ship's charts and could use them to find *his* world, but he couldn't even be bothered to look for Ariel's planet? She closed her eyes and fought the tears that burned behind her eyelids.

Ariel eventually opened her eyes and stared out into space once more, her emotions somewhat under control. She occasionally observed Ral, who looked excited as he moved around the room from station to station, continually conferring with him men.

He finally walked toward her and held out his hand. Hours had passed.

"We are not being pursued. They don't have anything faster than our ship, and we have been watching for them. We made a perfect escape. Come. We are going to the Anzon leader's sleeping quarters."

"All right." She let him pull her to her feet.

Ral retrieved his blanket-wrapped clothing by the door before they left the command center and walked down a long corridor. Ral eventually stopped by a door and opened it, stepping in first and dropping his clothes.

The lights automatically came on and Ariel glanced around the huge space, which looked fitted with every comfort the Anzons might have to offer.

"They put us in rock-hewn rooms with bed pallets." Ral looked pissed off. "Yet they lived in luxury."

Ariel studied the room closer. It had a living area similar to a living room, with comfortable-looking furniture, and there was an open bedroom section with a huge bed. One entire wall was a window to space. It was beautiful. It faced the sleeping area, and she knew gazing at it from the luxurious bed would be an experience in itself.

Ral reached for her, pulling her into his arms. "You will love Zorn."

She locked gazes with him. "You could find Earth if you wanted to."

"I can't let you return to Earth, Ariel."

"I don't understand why."

He held her tighter. "Yes...I could find your planet...but I can't let go of you now. I am in love with you. You are everything to me. We are bound."

"What does that mean? Bound?"

"It means I have taken you as mine until death. It means we are together until death. I have bound my life to yours."

"You mean we're married?"

"Married?"

"That means committed to each other until death. Though many Earthlings don't actually manage to commit themselves that long," she said wryly.

"Yes. Then that is what it means. You are bound to me, Ariel. I will never give you up."

"What is Argis?"

"My title."

"And Ral?"

"My name."

"Should I call you Argis Ral now, like everyone else?"

He grinned. "You are my bound. You need not call me by a title. Ever. When we were captured and taken, I ordered my people not to use my title in order to protect my identity. I was just one Zorn of many."

"If the Anzons captured you once, will they come back to your planet to get you again?"

"No. We were not taken from our home planet. We were taken from another we were visiting. It was our hunting planet. The Anzons made many mistakes with us. They thought we were not smart enough to work their technology, not even enough of a threat worthy of watching closely. We allowed them to think we were a docile race, fighting only when forced to do so. It worked in our favor, giving us access to escape."

"What is a hunt planet?"

"My kind take leisure trips on our hunt planet. It is a primitive planet without civilization. The ship that takes us there leaves us for a week. The Anzons thought we were a species with no technology, because we allow none on our hunting grounds, so that it might remain unspoiled. The Anzons are seriously learning how they underestimated us now." He chuckled.

"So they can't come after us on Zorn?"

Amusement lit Ral's incredible blue eyes. "No. We have ships far better than this and a defense system that would never allow them to get close to our home. When we return, I will have measures taken to defend our hunt planet from now on, when our people are visiting, so this never happens again."

Chapter Six

Ariel was nervous. She sat between Ral's thighs, staring at the planet they were approaching. Zorn wasn't a blue and white planet. Zorn was shades of red and had three large moons closely surrounding it. Ral nodded at one of his men.

"Open communications."

"Yes, Argis Ral."

"This is Argis Ral," he growled. "We have returned home. Alert Hyvin Berrr."

A male growled in response. "Argis Ral? Confirm your identity."

Ral issued more growls that the translator didn't interpret for Ariel. It was just harsh sounds to her ears.

"Welcome home, Argis Ral." The man sounded happy. "Hyvin Berrr will be very pleased. Your father has searched for you and our people without success."

"We have recently escaped our captors." Ral hugged Ariel. "We will need transports."

"Immediately, Argis Ral," the man said.

They put the ship in orbit over the planet, and Ariel couldn't stop staring at her new home. It looked so different from Earth. Not that she'd ever really seen Earth from space, just pictures and images from movies. Zorn was definitely different, seemed bigger than Earth, though again she couldn't be sure. She swallowed nervously.

"Are you all right, Ariel?" Ral softly growled in her ear.

"Yes. I'm just nervous. What is it like?"

He smiled as he held her tight. "You will like it. It is beautiful."

He still hadn't managed to tell her anything about his planet. For the last three weeks, while they'd traveled to Zorn, Ral had been extremely busy and constantly needed by his crew. He'd left her mostly alone in the leader's quarters, coming back late at night to sleep and make love to her. But he'd managed to successfully avoid all of her questions—and it was starting to concern her. To just say a planet was beautiful left a whole lot open.

Ral lifted both of them to their feet. He led her to the bowels of the ship, where most of his people had gathered. They looked exceptionally happy and excited, and Ral smiled and nodded at them as he pulled her closer.

"We are finally home. It has been too long since they have seen their families and friends."

Ariel missed her home and family too, but she offered a smile, though slightly sad. Ral was her world now. To go home meant she'd have to leave him. Despite only a month spent together, she already couldn't imagine life without him.

"They have sent transport ships to fly us to the planet. This ship is too large for our docking stations."

She eyed the ship around them. "What will happen to it?"

He smiled. "We'll keep it. They took us. We took their ship."

A loud sound startled Ariel. Ral chuckled. "A transport is docking." He motioned his head toward the far corner. "We will go first. My father, Hyvin Berrr, will be very anxious to see me, as will my brothers."

She gripped his hand tighter, staring up at his face. "How will they feel about me?"

"We are bound. They will have to accept it."

"Can't your father unbind us? You said he was leader of this world."

Ral frowned. "He won't."

Dread suddenly hit Ariel.

Ral didn't say the man *couldn't* unbind them. He'd used the word *won't*, which implied it was possible.

What if his father wanted Ariel out of Ral's life? What would become of her then?

The doors he'd indicated slid open and large Zorn men dressed in black uniforms stepped out. Ral smiled. He walked forward, pulling Ariel along behind him as he closed the space between himself and the newcomers.

"Argernon! You came all this way to see me." Ral released Ariel to yank a man into a bear hug. Ariel noted the resemblance between them.

Argernon kept his smile in place as he released Ral. "You look good, brother. We feared you were dead."

Ral chuckled. "I am too mean to die." He turned, reaching for Ariel and bringing her forward.

Ariel stared up at the large Zorn, whose eyes widened as he stared back at her. His mouth opened but immediately slammed shut. His gaze flew to Ral. "She smells strongly of you."

"This is Ariel. I am bound to her."

Horror instantly lit Argernon's features. "You bound to an *enemy*?"

Ral growled. "She is no enemy."

"She is one of your captors."

"*No*. She was taken from her world, just as we were taken from ours."

Argernon still looked pretty angry. "She is otherworld. You cannot be bound to one from another world. Father will not allow it."

Ral growled viciously. "It is done. She is mine. We are bound."

Argernon took a step back. He put up his hands. "I will let you take it up with father." His gaze lowered to Ariel. "She is too small and pale."

"She is *mine*," Ral snarled again at his brother. "No one will take her from me."

Argernon looked concerned. "Is she breeding compatible? Can she carry your offspring?"

Ral hesitated. "I do not know, nor do I care."

Argernon sighed deeply. "Let us go. Father has a strong desire to see you." He glanced at Ariel. "Can she even understand us?"

"Yes." Ral focused his attention on her too. "Ariel, will you speak to my brother please, to see if Zorn translators work with your language?"

Ariel swallowed. "Hello, Argernon. It's nice to meet you."

Argernon frowned. His gaze slid to Ral. He shook his head. "I cannot understand her. And she speaks too softly. She does not speak like us."

Irritation made Ral frown. "We will have someone work on this. The translators the Anzon fitted us with allow Ariel and I to communicate. We'll have to modify our Zorn translators for her language."

"This is not acceptable!" Argernon growled. "You brought a woman home who can't even speak or understand our language!"

Ariel glanced at Ral. "I can understand him."

Ral nodded at her. "Good."

"What did she say?" Argernon asked.

"She can understand you perfectly. Let's go. Contact someone and have them work on our translators immediately. I want my bound woman able to speak so *all* can understand her, not just the Zorn on this ship."

Argernon looked furious. His glowing blue eyes narrowed on Ariel for a second. She felt uneasy under his direct gaze. He snapped an affirmative response before the man spun around to stomp to the door he'd come through.

The transport was about the size of an Earth bus. Ral pulled Ariel onto his lap, belting them in as other Zorn filled the seats. The doors closed and then they were flying toward the planet. When they hit Zorn's atmosphere, the transporter shook, making for a rough ride, but Ral just chuckled at Ariel's obvious fear and held her tighter. He nuzzled her cheek with his and whispered into the wrong ear, softly growling at her. She didn't bother reminding him that she couldn't understand him in that ear; she knew the gist of what he'd said. He was assuring her that they were safe.

The transport didn't have windows, so she didn't get to see anything until it touched down with a small bump. Ral unfastened them from the seat then took her hand to lead her outside.

She had a fleeting moment to realize she was able to breathe in Zorn's atmosphere, before her focus snagged on a group of men standing a short distance from the transport.

Ariel knew they were Ral's father and brothers immediately. His father looked so much like an older version of Ral, introductions weren't necessary. The four younger men who surrounded their father all shared a strong family resemblance as well.

Ral kept a tight hold of her hand until he reached out to his father, gripping the older man in a bear hug.

Ariel watched Ral hug each of his family members. The men looked really happy to have him back. She didn't move an inch until one of Ral's brothers turned his attention to her.

He frowned and stared at Ral. "What is she?"

Ral pulled back from the last brother's embrace. He turned, smiling, and reached for Ariel. "This is Ariel. I am bound to her."

The old man unleashed a piercing roar.

Ral's father was obviously furious.

Ariel gasped, almost falling on her ass as she stumbled back to distance herself from the man. Ral caught her around the waist to haul her against his body, his arm locking her to his side.

He snarled at his father. "What was that for?"

"You are not bound to *that*!" Ral's father snarled back.

Ral's mouth tightened into a grim line. "She's from Earth. She's human. She was taken from her planet by the Anzons, the same ones who kidnapped me and our people. I have bound to her. She is mine. Never roar at her again, Father."

"She's small and weak! Look at her skin. It is pale."

Hyvin Berrr glared at Ariel as he spoke. If looks could kill, she knew she'd be taking her last breath. This man ruled Zorn, according to Ral. If the older man wanted her dead, she had a sinking feeling she wouldn't have much time left to live.

"She is brave and beautiful. I do not care what you think of her species. I have bound her." Ral faced off against his father. His body was tense and his hold on Ariel almost bruising. "I will *not* let her be taken from me."

His father shot a vicious look at Ariel. "What kind of hold does she have on you?" He turned his head to stare at a Zorn woman. "Take her to medical. I want to know if she is doing something to my son to make him lose his head."

Ral growled. "No!"

Argernon got between father and son. "Let her be examined. You will be at her side, Ral. It will make Father see she has not bewitched you with some otherworld magic. You can also have her translator evaluated to see if it can be tuned so others besides you can understand her."

Ral was breathing hard and he was obviously still pissed off. He jerked a nod at Argernon. He glared at his father. "If you try to remove her from me, I will take that ship back into space and we will go to her world. You will lose me forever."

Ral grabbed Ariel's hand and stormed away. She had to run to keep up with his longer strides. She got one last glimpse of Hyvin Berrr's furious face before he was no longer in sight.

They followed the Zorn woman toward medical. It wasn't very far but Ariel eyed her surroundings during the short trip.

Zorn *was* beautiful. The towering buildings were mostly black and the sky had a red tint, reminding her of a sunset at home, but with all of the sky a light red. The ground beneath their feet was a darker red, and the grass was a vibrant purple. They walked over a small bridge and she paused.

Ral stopped with her, following the direction of her stare. "What is it?"

"Your water is a dark purple."

"What color is water on your planet?"

"Clear, mostly, but our oceans are blue."

He rubbed her hand in his. "It sounds nice."

"I'm just glad I can breathe. I was worried about that."

He chuckled. "I wasn't. We breathe the same. Let's go."

The Zorn woman was waiting, her interest fixed on Ariel. She looked at her like Ariel as if she were a bug she'd like to squash.

Ariel sighed. "I don't think your people like me."

"You look different, but you are beautiful."

"*You* think so."

"They think so as well. You are simply different, and they haven't seen such pale skin before."

"What is she saying?" the Zorn woman asked softly.

Ral turned his attention to the woman. "She thinks you don't like her. I was explaining that you are just curious."

The woman nodded. "She can understand us, but I cannot understand her?"

"Her Anzon translator allows her to understand our language," Ral explained.

The woman nodded again. "She speaks so softly and strangely but it is pleasant to the ear."

With that, they continued inside the medical building, where they were taken to the second floor. The woman smiled at Ariel, her expression looking slightly forced.

"I am a healer and a scientist. Do you understand me? I am Ahhu."

Ariel nodded.

The woman looked relieved. She addressed Ral. "Will you stay so you can translate for me?"

"I will not leave my Ariel's side."

"Can you have her remove her clothing? I would like to examine her."

Ariel tensed. "Now I feel like a bug under a microscope."

"What does that mean?" Ral arched his eyebrow.

She met his curious gaze. "I feel like a science experiment. Is that a better description?"

Ral pulled her into his arms to give her a hug. "I know this is difficult for you, Ariel. I am sorry."

She nodded against his chest and let him comfort her for a moment, then pulled back. "It's all right." She removed her clothing, which were more of Ral's garments, the only things she still had to wear. Ahhu stared at her with open curiosity. Ariel flushed but otherwise stood still as the woman's gaze raked over her body.

"You have bred her." Ahhu glanced at Ral. "Correct?"

"Yes. I told you I bound her."

Ahhu hesitated. "How is she physically different from our women?"

"Besides her obvious looks?" Ral growled.

"Besides."

"It's all right," Ariel sighed. "Don't get mad."

He *was* mad. Ariel could see it. Ral glared at the Zorn woman. "Her *unis* is in the front."

"I don't understand."

"Her *unis* is in the front, exposed between her thighs when spread."

The Zorn scientist's gaze lowered down Ariel. "May I please see this?"

Ariel knew Ahhu had to examine her, but she still felt embarrassment. Nevertheless, she climbed onto an exam table. She spread her thighs but she closed her eyes, so she didn't have to watch herself being stared at.

When a hand touched her down below, she instinctually tried to jerk away, her eyes flying open, but it was just Ral. Relieved, she instantly relaxed. He spread her nether lips with his fingers to better expose her sex. Ral's gaze locked with Ariel's. He didn't look at the scientist.

"Look but do not touch her, Ahhu," Ral warned. "You are making her uncomfortable—and you will treat her with the respect of my bound woman."

The woman dipped her head in a nod. "Of course, Argis Ral."

Ariel saw the woman staring at every exposed inch of her as Ral explained Ariel's "pleasure center", briefly and without attempting to touch her. Ahhu reached for something.

Ral instantly growled. He looked furious. "No."

Ahhu froze. "I simply wanted to document."

"You will not take documentation of my woman's sexual center to share with other scientists. Put that down *now*," he snarled. "No other male sees my woman like this but me."

Ahhu put the electronic device down but moved closer to study Ariel. She seemed fascinated. "Her color is different. She's pink."

"She is softer inside, too." Ral released Ariel's labia and slid his palm up to cover her sex, cupping her with one large hand. "You have seen enough."

The woman backed up. "Can she enter your mind? Any signs of telepathic abilities?"

"No." Ral helped Ariel sit up. He handed her clothes back and started to help her dress. "She has no abilities that could control me."

Ahhu was frowning. "Then why did you bound to her?"

Ral lifted Ariel off the table to help her put on her pants. "Seeing her was enough. I was drawn to her fragile beauty. She smelled good, and I wanted her intensely. When we were alone, I got to know her very well. I knew she was mine to keep. I knew she was the woman I wanted bound to."

The scientist studied Ral. "She pleases you?"

Ral nodded. Now that Ariel was dressed, Ral's anger seemed to dissipate. "More than I have ever been pleased in my life." He looked down at Ariel. "Let her look at your implant." He eyed Ahhu. "Can you download the program and load her language into our translators, so all Zorn can understand her? How long will that take?"

Ahhu walked to a wall and got another device before returning. "Tell her to sit."

Ariel sat before Ral could speak. "Please remind her that I can understand her just fine."

Ral chuckled. "She can understand you, Ahhu."

The woman approached and ran the device over the wrong ear. Ariel pointed. "This one."

She moved the device and ran it over Ariel's right ear, reading the small screen. She frowned as she looked at Ral. "Let me see yours."

Ahhu scanned both ears on Ral and frowned harder. "I see the Anzon translator in your left ear. I would like to remove the otherworld implants from you both, Argis Ral. We do not know what their technology can do. It could be dangerous."

"No. I won't allow it."

"Your father is going to order all of the implants removed from the other Zorn. We do not know if they contain tracking devices, or even harmful weaponry…"

"What are the chances?"

The woman hesitated. "Good. Remember our history."

It was Ariel's turn to frown as she met Ral's gaze. "We won't be able to able to understand each other, will we?"

"No. The Zorn translators obviously don't know your language."

"At least let us remove it for testing. We might be able to download their program to adapt our translators," Ahhu urged.

Ral frowned. "Remove the implants from our people and test those."

"They *all* must be removed, Argis Ral. I swear to you that I will work very hard to find a way for our translators to work for your bound woman."

Ral growled menacingly. There was no translation for *that* sound. "Leave us and lock the door. We need some time together."

Ahhu nodded. "The other recovered Zorn are coming in right now. I'll remove their implants first." She left the room.

Ral met Ariel's eyes. "We need to do this. She could be right. We have had something similar happen before to some of our warriors, who were captured by otherworld species. They were given alien implants that released poisons that killed them all. It happened days after they escaped."

Ariel was horrified. But she said, "We've been traveling for three weeks."

"We have been aboard *their* ship, where their own safety measures may have kept us from harm. But we are out of range of any signals the ship might send out, now that we are on our planet. It is safer if we do this. I won't take the risk with your life or mine."

She sighed, her heart heavy. "I understand."

Ral reached for her. "It doesn't matter if we can talk or not." He pulled her into his arms. "We know how we feel about each other."

"We do."

"I will take care of you. It shouldn't be too difficult for them to create a working translator. We have the Anzons' ship, as well with their programs. We'll find your language and upload it to our translators. We can do this together, Ariel."

"We can do this," she echoed, hoping they were both right.

"It won't be long."

Ariel stared up into his eyes and cupped his face with her hands. "I love you." One of her hands lowered from his face to his heart. "I love you so much, Ral." She touched his chest. She wasn't exactly sure his heart lay beneath her palm, but she heard a thump there under her ear when they slept. "My heart to yours."

Ral smiled. "I am in love with you too, Ariel."

She was a little afraid of the concept of not being able to talk to Ral, even if just for a few days. Ariel wondered if he was putting up a brave front as well. She just had to have some faith that they'd make it work somehow.

Ariel forced a smile that she didn't feel. "Just don't feed me hot things that make my mouth burn. I won't be able to understand you when you describe my food choices now."

He laughed. "I'll remember. I'll take good care of you."

Chapter Seven

Ariel already hated not being able to talk to Ral.

He had led her outside of the medical building, where a vehicle with a driver waited after their implants had been removed. They'd left the city for a forested area. Ral's home was at the edge of what looked like a village. Other large homes were within sight, but they were distanced enough that there was ample privacy.

Ral had a beautiful home, though Zorn houses were not like any back on Earth. His home was made out of a pretty red stone. The walls were smooth to the touch, as if they had been polished. He had wooded furniture but the colors didn't come from any types of trees Arial had ever seen. The wood was in shades of red and deep purples—which seemed to be the two dominant colors on the planet, though some furniture was black. The cloth material on the couches—as well as most of the Zorn clothing—was thick, soft cotton-like blends.

Ral gave Ariel a tour of each room in his house. He smiled at her as he led her to a large bedroom last. He softly growled as he swept her into his arms and took them both to the bed. He growled at her again. She knew he was talking, and wished so badly that she could understand him.

Their gazes met as Ral pinned her under him. He touched her throat with his finger and ran it up to her mouth.

"You want to hear what I sound like when I talk without the translator on?"

Nodding his head, Ral grinned. He either understood what she was asking or maybe he just wanted to encourage her to keep speaking.

"I love your house. It's bigger than I thought it would be, and I like the darker tones. I never really enjoyed red or thought there were so many shades of the color, but I love them here. I also never thought purple would be in a straight man's home, but we're not on Earth. Purple is definitely sexy around a hunk like you."

Ral chuckled. No translation was needed for that sound. His amazing eyes sparkled with amusement as his head lowered. He brushed his lips over hers. Ariel wrapped her arms around his neck to pull him closer. She was addicted to sex with the man, pretty much since the moment she'd met him. They had no problem communicating when they touched. They both knew exactly what they were saying as the kiss deepened. They wanted each other.

A loud buzz sounded.

Ral's body tensed as he broke the kiss, reluctantly pulling his mouth from hers. He snarled something as he climbed off her, eyeing her body with a long hungry look. Holding his palm out to her, he turned around, walking out of the bedroom. She stayed in bed, as his hand gesture indicated.

Minutes passed—then Ariel heard a loud shattering sound, like glass being smashed, followed by vicious snarls.

She jumped off the bed to run out of the bedroom, fear for Ral's safety swamping her. Something was wrong.

She came to a halt as she saw the living room.

Ral was facing off with an angry-looking Zorn woman. The female was tall, muscular, and attractive. Dark brown hair flowed down her back all the way to her knees. Most of her athletic body was showing in the dress she wore, which was low cut at her breasts and ended high on her shapely legs.

Both she and Ral were oblivious to Ariel.

The woman grabbed Ral's arm with a snarl and he slapped her hand away, snarling something back that, even to Ariel's ears, didn't sound nice. The woman snatched her hand back as they glared at each other.

Then the woman's nostrils flared—and she snapped her head in Ariel's direction with an intense glare.

Ariel didn't need a translator to understand the woman hated her. Rage was evident in every line of her expression.

The woman snarled and took a step in Ariel's direction.

Ral moved and got in the woman's path, snarling back at the woman. Ariel understood from his tone that he was pissed. She couldn't see the woman anymore, with Ral's huge body between them, but when he stopped snarling, the woman growled back. They were obviously arguing.

Ral pointed to the door with a particularly nasty snarl.

Nope, Ariel thought. *No translation needed.* The woman was clearly angry that Ral had brought Ariel home, and wanted the Zorn woman to leave. But she didn't.

Instead, she lunged at Ral.

He took a single step back when the woman attacked him, grabbing her wrists as she tried to punch him.

He threw the woman away from him and she landed hard on her ass. Ral snarled, again pointing at the front door.

The woman shot Ariel another death glare as she softly growled something. She got to her knees and reached for her hem.

In shock, Ariel watched the woman yank the dress over her head. It looked like Zorn females didn't wear undergarments, because the woman was now completely naked.

Zorn women weren't that different, Ariel noted. Her breast looked the same, for the most part. She thought her groin might be slightly different, but it was hard to tell. The woman obviously didn't own a much-needed razor. She gave new meaning to the word "bush".

The woman's gaze locked on Ral as she dropped to her hands and knees. She softly growled at him, lowering her head, her arms bent at the elbows. She lowered her breasts to the floor, putting her ass high in the air as she spread her thighs about a foot apart.

"Oh, hell no," Ariel gasped. Once again, she had zero need for a translator. The woman was offering herself to Ral.

Ral turned to frown at Ariel. She met his eyes.

He pointed to the bedroom.

Pain shot through Ariel, hard. Was he going to accept the bitch's offer?

He wanted Ariel to return to their room. That was clear.

She shook her head at him, feeling a burst of emotions. Jealousy and hurt were the strongest; they hit her first. Anger and shock came in at a close second.

Ral took a deep breath. He continued to frown at Ariel, and pointed again to the bedroom.

"Fuck you," she said softly. She shook her head no, crossing her arms. "If you touch that bitch, I'm out of here."

Ariel hesitated before she pointed at the woman, then the door. Next, she pointed at Ral and then the woman, with a questioning look. Finally, she pointed to herself then the door. She hoped he understood what she meant. She let her anger show. She even growled at him.

Ral now just looked confused.

Ariel stormed over to him. She looked up to stare into his eyes, putting her hands over both her heart and Ral's. She pointed to the woman, then to him, and she shook her head viciously.

He knew what *that* meant.

Hot tears fill her eyes. If he touched that woman, she'd leave him. She didn't care what happened to her out on his planet. She wasn't going to stay with a man who'd fuck another woman.

Ral's frown softened. He pointed to the woman, shaking his head no. He touched his chest and then hers. His eyes left Ariel's to look down at the naked woman bent over on the floor. He growled something at her.

In response, the woman snarled as she lifted her chest from the floor. She looked pissed off as hell as she reached for her discarded dress, yanking it over her head and down her body as she got to her feet.

This time, she lunged at *Ariel*.

Ral moved fast. His arm wrapped around Ariel and jerked her out of reach of the furious woman, holding the Zorn female off with one hand. He dropped Ariel to her feet behind him before swiftly turning and shoving the woman toward the door.

She lunged for Ariel again, but Ral was obviously done being nice.

He grabbed the woman by the throat and lifted her straight off the floor, stomped to the door, jerked it open, dropped the uninjured woman outside and slammed the door shut, engaging some sort of lock.

Ral turned slowly, his blue eyes meeting Ariel's before he advanced.

Ariel gasped when Ral grabbed her. He softly growled as he hoisted her into his arms.

Outside, the woman pounded on the door. She rang the annoying bell over and over. Ral ignored the noise as he carried Ariel into their bedroom, turning to kick the door shut. It almost muted out the sounds of the woman attacking his front door and doorbell.

He walked to the bed, easing Ariel to her feet.

She undressed as quickly as Ral did, relief flooding.

He wanted her. He'd kicked the other woman out of his house. He'd chosen Ariel.

Ral climbed on the bed and flipped onto his back. A slow smile spread across his lips as he softly growled at her, patting his thighs. He gave her a look she knew well. Ariel on top was his favorite position.

She climbed on the bed. Straddling his hips, she kept his erection behind her for now, grinning as she ran her fingertips over his chest. The man had a body she wanted to lick, so she didn't hesitate. She lowered her head and started at his right nipple.

Groans were also universal, as was Ral's heavy breathing after a few minutes of Ariel's tongue and teeth.

Ral gripped her hips, lifting her, surprising her as always with his strength as he lowered her on his body so she was right over his cock. She spread her thighs a little wider, so wet and ready as he eased himself into her. Ariel threw her head back moaning as she settled down on him, Ral seated deep inside her. The sensation was amazing.

Ariel rode him at a slow pace. She twisted her hips as she moved up and down, so every thick inch of him hit nerves that drove her passion level higher and higher.

She locked her gaze with his and Ral ran his hands over her body, down to the vee of her thighs to finger her clit. He brushed the sensitive nub gently as he growled at her. The look in his eyes told her that whatever he was saying, it was good—though she desperately missed hearing his words.

But she knew he thought she was hot and tight. She knew he loved the way she felt as her body gripped his cock. She squeezed her muscles tighter when she moved faster.

Ariel came with a shout, her climax hitting her when Ral rubbed her clit faster with his fingertips, applying just the right amount of pressure.

Ral pulsed and throbbed hard inside her when he ejaculated. She loved the way he felt, coming inside her.

She collapsed on his chest and Ral let his hands run up and down her spine. Ariel adored his rough-textured hands on her bare skin. She shivered, and Ral started to harden again inside her. The man had a crazy rapid recovery time.

Zorn men were a lot like humans in some ways but so different in others, and that was one of them. Ral had the stamina of at least five human men.

He gently rolled them over until he had her pinned to the bed beneath him.

Ariel grinned up at him. "I love you."

Ral tilted his head.

Ariel touched her heart and then his. A grin spread across his lips.

He shifted his hips and then drove into her, thrusting fast and hard. Ariel locked her legs high around his waist so her heels dug into his flexing ass. She clung to him and rolled her hips as he pounded into her. Ecstasy flowed through her body, her inner muscles quivering around his cock, and she screamed out again minutes later as she came a second time.

Ral swiftly followed and collapsed on top of her, careful not to crush her with his full weight. He kissed her neck, a growl rumbling from him.

She had to admit, when he softly growled like that into her skin, it turned her on as much as his loving words did. She caressed his hair, letting her fingers slide into his thick tresses. She loved his long hair. She never thought she'd find really long hair sexy on a man, but everything about Ral was intensely hot.

He climbed off her then smiled as he held out his hand. She gripped it and let him lift her off his bed. He led her silently into the bathroom, where they showered together. He seemed to love to run his soapy hands all over her body.

Soon, their touches were doing more than just cleansing. Her body heated up and she grinned as Ral grew aroused. She let her soapy hands run down his stomach to wash every muscle along the way and finally her hand grasped the hard flesh pointed at her. Both of her hands closed over him as she explored with her fingers.

Ral leaned back against the wall and his eyes narrowed with lust. Ariel watched his expression as she rubbed him and let her fingernails lightly rake his balls. Ral's eyes closed and a moan escaped. He tilted his head back. His lips parted so she could see his sharp teeth—those teeth that had once frightened her. Now she knew the wonderful feel of them raking over her skin.

Ral came with a roar, jerking with the violence of his release. Ariel smiled at him when he finally opened his eyes. His grin was wide and happy as he stared down at her. He reached up and cupped her face with both hands before lowering his head to brush his lips over hers. They eventually parted, breathless, and finished their shower.

Back in Ral's bedroom, Ariel was surprised to learn the woman outside still hadn't given up. Irritation surged as she got dressed, the doorbell still going off incessantly, with the occasional thump from the woman kicking or punching the door.

Ral eyed Ariel. He touched his heart and then hers before walking out of the bedroom. Ariel followed.

She was a little stunned as she watched Ral open the front door and move out of the way. The woman stormed into the house, snarling. Her dark eyes narrowed, hatred poured from their depths as she shot yet another glare at Ariel. The woman snapped her head in Ral's direction and she spoke to him softly.

Ral shut the door. His gaze went to Ariel, and he touched his chest before pointing at her. He was telling her that he loved her.

Ariel frowned and she looked from him to the woman. If he loved her, then why in the hell was that bitch in their home?

The woman dropped to her knees and she reached for her hem again. She started to tug up her dress—and Ariel saw red. Rage filling her, compounded by her frustration at not being able to communicate.

If Ral thought he could have them both, he was about to get a serious reality check.

Ariel stormed to the front door. She was leaving. She didn't care what his people decided to do with her. She'd probably end up at the medical center like a guinea pig, but it would be better than watching Ral touch another woman.

Opening the front door, she darted out and slammed it shut behind her. She halted briefly, staring around her at the alien landscape, and then started walking toward the road, fighting back tears. Ral had brought her to his world, refused to let her go home, and now he seemed to be discarding her—or at the very least, expecting her to share him.

Okay, maybe discarded wasn't the right word, she admitted. He hadn't asked her to leave.

No. He'd just let a naked woman into their home.

She heard a roar seconds before the front door was torn open behind her. Ariel didn't turn around. She also didn't run, even though she was a little scared. It sounded like Ral was pretty pissed off.

Well, too damn bad. She was furious with him, too, and hurt by his actions. She wasn't the sharing kind. She'd be damned if she stayed with a two-timing son of a bitch.

She made it to the street before Ral grabbed her arm and spun her around to face him.

Ariel saw the confusion and rage on Ral's face. He spoke to her, but she shrugged her shoulders. "I don't understand a damn thing you've said, and I know you don't understand me either, but go to hell. I won't stand there while you fuck another woman! Screw you, buddy. I'm out of here! And don't glare down at me like that and act all pissy. I don't have a naked man on his hands and knees in my house, you jerk."

He looked frustrated as hell. Ariel yanked hard to free her arm as she turned away from him to start walking away again.

Ral roared in rage seconds before Ariel's world turned upside down—literally.

Then all she could do was gasp as she found herself once again tossed over his shoulder, two arms locked tightly around her thighs as he stormed back to the house. He'd left the front door wide open.

He gently put her down on her feet in the living room. Ariel took in the room once she was right-side up. The bitch was still on her knees on the floor, still naked, and obviously still waiting for Ral to fuck her.

Ral glared down at Ariel as he touched his heart and then brushed his fingertips over Ariel's chest.

"You love me? You want to remind me we're bound? What in the hell does that mean? Damn you, Ral!" She pointed to the naked woman on the floor and shook her head as she yelled at him. "No way in hell are you having us both, you jackass! If screwing around is your planet's version of a relationship then just forget it. Let your father unbound us. I won't stay!"

Ral growled softly. He spun and walked to some sort of communication device on the wall. It looked kind of similar to a wireless phone. She listened to him talk to someone, since the device broadcast both sides of the conversation. He spoke to a female. Minutes later, he looked frustrated. He glanced at Ariel as he made another call to a male. When he hung up, he let his attention shift to the naked woman. He growled something at her.

Whatever he said, the woman wasn't happy. She shot Ariel a murderous look as she finally got off her knees and put her dress on a second time.

Was Ral sending her away? Did he actually understand Ariel's I'm-out-of-here-if-you-touch-her message?

Clearly not. The woman didn't leave. Instead, she headed toward the kitchen.

Ariel clenched her teeth. Ral moved to stand in front of her, his gaze softening as he rubbed her arms with his large hands. It was a comforting gesture, but Ariel wasn't placated. She couldn't understand what was going on.

She glared up at Ral before jerking out of his hold.

He frowned at her, reaching for her again. His hand was gentle as it gripped her arm. He led her to the front door.

Shock tore through Ariel. Was he going to kick *her* out now? He'd just chased after her and carried her back into the house!

He pulled her outside and shut the door behind them. They walked toward the street, where she saw one of the Zorn vehicles approach.

Pain sliced through her. Ral was sending her away. The vehicle stopped and Ral kept hold of her arm as he opened the back door. He gently pushed her toward the vehicle.

Ariel fought tears as she climbed inside the back of the transport. She sat stiffly—but gasped as Ral pushed at her to move over. He climbed inside with her, shutting the door and closing them in together. Ariel stared at him, still clueless about what was going on. But it seemed clear he wasn't sending her away.

He touched his heart and then hers before pulling her onto his lap to hold her as he spoke to the driver. The vehicle took off, Ariel cuddled in his arms. She had no idea where they were going, but at least they were together. She felt relief that he wasn't just sending her away, but was still confused, angry, and she wanted answers.

Ral held her while they took the long drive back to the city. When they parked, she recognized the building the driver had stopped in front of as the medical center. Ral lifted her from his lap as he eased out of the vehicle. He held out his hand and Ariel took it. She desperately hoped they had their translators fixed so she could be refitted with one. She really wanted to talk to Ral.

Inside, she saw other Zorn, and as usual, Ral kept hold of her as they moved down the hallway. She spotted the same woman who'd examined her walking toward them. Ahhu smiled at Ral but just gave Ariel a blank look. Ral growled at the woman. She growled back. Ariel didn't understand a damn word, of course; could only stand there wishing she knew what the hell was going on.

Ahhu turned started back down the corridor, Ral and Ariel both following the Zorn woman.

Ahhu showed them into a different exam room this time. Ariel watched the woman walk to what looked like maybe their version of a computer. Ral shut the door firmly behind them, closing the three of them in the room, and spoke to the doctor as she worked at the console. Finally, Ahhu turned to face them.

"Can you understand me now?" She stared at Ariel.

Joy hit her instantly. "Yes!"

Ral chuckled. "We can understand you too. I've missed your words." He grinned down at her.

"This is a program from the implant device we took off you," Ahhu explained. "The *conis* is running it for us. We haven't worked it out fully so we don't have a new implant to give either of you yet, but in here, you can talk."

Ral glared at the woman. "Damn it, Ahhu. We need to be able to understand each other at all times. To be unable is causing us problems."

"I can copy the program so it can be run in a room in your home, so you may communicate. It is tricky to try to implement a foreign program into our implant translators. The device doesn't want to read it. The only reason it works on the *conis* is because it can run most any program."

"*Conis*?" Ariel asked.

Ahhu pointed to the computer-looking device.

Ariel nodded. "Got it." She eyed Ral. "Do you have a *conis* at home? I don't remember seeing one."

"I can get one." He waved a hand at Ahhu. "Leave us, please. Get me a copy of that program. Tell Abroo I need a *conis* immediately to take home with us."

Ahhu hesitated. "While you are here, I need to run more tests."

"No," Ral snarled.

"Your father has ordered them, Ral. He is greatly concerned."

Ral snarled again. There was no translation but it came across as "no fucking way" to Ariel. "He need not concern himself."

"I am simply doing as ordered. Let me run the tests. It will set his mind at ease. He's ordered all the otherworld species off of our planet, Argis Ral. If you refuse, I'm certain he will order her gone as well. Let me run the tests to prove to him that she is no danger to your health and well-being."

Rage hit Ral's face. "He's ordered our men to give up their off-world bounds?"

Ahhu hesitated. "None of the others bound to those women, Ral. Only you. They just shared sex. The other males were willing to give up those women. They are working now to find their planets, to return them to their home worlds."

"I will not give her up. If he orders her off Zorn, then I will go live on her planet. Leave us." He paused. "What tests do you wish to do now? I won't allow her to be pained in any way."

Ahhu walked to cabinets along one wall. She removed a few things before crossing to a table. "Your father has demanded I make sure she does not have sexual control over you. I need her sex fluids, in order to be certain they aren't working as a drug in your system. I will also need sex fluids from you as well, to see if her fluids cause any other reaction in your body."

Ral growled. "Fine."

"You can't mix the fluids. Will this be a problem?" Ahhu glanced at Ariel. "Does she *have* fluids?"

"Yes. Get out. I'll take care of the testing. Lock the door on your way out."

Ahhu nodded and left the room. It locked with a loud click from the other side. Ral sighed as he turned around, his full attention on Ariel.

Chapter Eight

"Why did you try to leave my home? What have I done to anger you?"

Ariel crossed her arms over her chest as she eyed him back. "I don't share. I thought bound meant loyalty. As in, you wouldn't fuck other women. I will leave, Ral. If you touch that woman, I'm so gone."

He cocked his head. "I see."

"You *see*? That's all you have to say? Let me tell you something, Ral. I'm human. You're Zorn. I know there are some differences, but I will *not* be with a man who has sex with other women. It won't happen. If you want to fuck that bitch...that woman...you go right ahead, but you won't be touching me anymore."

"This wasn't an issue while we were prisoners. Women were too rare. On my world, it is acceptable for a male to have sex with different females. But I did not invite her to our home. My father gave her to me. He wants me bound with her instead. I told her I wasn't interested. I did not wish to have her, Ariel."

"You let her back in after you kicked her out. She took off her dress and you didn't make her put it back on!"

"Many of my kind are comfortable naked. It is not an uncommon or unheard of thing, even in someone else's home."

"She goes, or I do, Ral. It's that simple. I'm really hurt that you'd even consider it." She moved away from him to stare out the window. "You've really hurt me deeply." She regarded him over her shoulder. "How would you feel if I had sex with another man?"

Ral snarled. In seconds he was on her, gripping her arms to spin her around to face him. "I would kill him!"

"That's how *I* feel, damn you! That rage you're feeling right now when you even *think* about another man touching me? I feel the same rage when I think about you with other women."

"Our culture is different...but I understand." His gaze softened. "I promise you no other women. I didn't mean to harm you, Ariel. I meant no hurt to you. I don't want her. You are the one I want in my bed. I did not think you would find it offensive that she was naked. Now I know. No more unclothed females in our home."

Ariel stared up at him. "Did you want to have sex with her?"

He didn't look away. "I did not. I told her no, and I *meant* no. You are the only one who makes me hard, Ariel. You are different from women of my world and I am addicted to those differences. To touch any woman but you would be..." He hesitated. "Not worth my time or of any interest. Was that clear for you to understand? You are the only female I want to touch."

"She goes."

He hesitated. "She was given to me. If I kick her out, she will be without a home. She will starve, or be harmed without protection. It would be cruel."

"Then give her to someone who will take care of her. I don't want her living with us."

He caressed her cheek. "I will give her to someone else. Good plan. We do need house help, but I will find a very old female to do the home work. She will stay in a room far from ours. Then there will be no doubt that I do not want to have sex with her. And older females do not walk around naked. They get too cold."

"You didn't have help before."

His expression turned guarded. "I did. My home help was ordered to leave before I took you home."

Ariel eyed him.

He looked away briefly before letting his gaze find hers again. He looked slightly embarrassed. "I had two females who shared my bed. I do not wish to make you angry or hurt, but I was unbound before you. I have a strong sex drive. I gave them to one of my brothers. They would not have been happy to leave my bed so that I could share it with you. I have no intention of having sex with others now that I have bound to you, Ariel. You have ruined me for other women."

She smiled. "Good."

He laughed. "House help will be useful. You don't know how to prepare our food. And the females do the shopping, but I would not send you out to shop. I would worry. We would have great sex but we would starve."

"We can't have that."

"Are you all right with me having two women before you?"

"I'm not overly thrilled. I'm glad you got rid of them." She moved closer to him, her hands opening on his shirt to rub his chest. "I mean it though. If you touch another woman, I'll leave you, Ral. I will be loyal to you but I expect it back."

"That is a promise I can easily make to you."

She grinned. "It's a deal then." She hesitated. "What exactly makes us bound? Is it like a ceremony?"

"I do not pull out of you."

"I'm not sure I understand."

"I give you my seed. I plant it inside you."

"Oh." She frowned. "Don't you do that with other women? I mean, haven't you?"

"No. We pull out to spill our seed. I do not do that with you. I empty my seed deep within your body. It makes us bound." His hand rubbed her belly. "You drank my seed as well. Our women do not drink our seed. They move away before seed is spilled. I told you they do not take us inside their mouths—but you do." He grinned widely. "It is amazing."

"So that makes us bound."

He nodded. "You are bound to me. You are offered my offspring with my seed."

"If I'm able to have offspring with you."

He nodded. "If you can. Time will tell us if you are able to have my seed grow inside you."

The thought of getting pregnant with Ral's baby didn't terrify her. It should have. Ariel smiled up at him. "I'm glad we can talk."

"When we leave, we will take the program and they will get me a *conis* so we can communicate in our bedroom."

"That's the one place we *don't* need to talk." She laughed.

"We will do their tests and leave." He backed away as he released her. "Undress and lie down."

Ariel eyed the room uneasily.

"We will not be interrupted."

Ariel stripped out of her clothes. Ral did the same. She glanced at the exam table with a grin. "It is a little small for both of us."

"Only one of us needs to fit on it. They want our fluids." He dropped his gaze. "I will make you very wet and take a sample for them. You may put me in your mouth to coax my seed. I will warn you before I find my release so you can pull away."

"Who's first?" Ariel appreciated his muscular, naked body. She loved to see every hard inch of him. Her gaze lowered to his major hard-on and she grinned. "You look very eager. Should you be first?"

"No. I will only get hard again from your taste. I would want you after."

Ariel smiled wider. "Good." She yanked a cushion from the exam table. She dropped it on the floor, sinking to her knees, and wiggled her finger at him. "Come here."

He moved forward. Ariel gripped his cock to guide him even closer. She wrapped one hand around his hard flesh as the other one gently massaged his balls.

Ral growled. "You first."

She shook her head. "*You* first. Then it will be my turn."

"I will want you."

"We'll be done with their tests. Then you can take me."

She saw strong desire change his eyes. His cock jumped in her hand. "Another good plan."

"I have my moments. So where is that collection cup?"

He turned at his waist to reach for it. He opened the container and sat it on the exam table a foot from Ariel.

She lowered her head, opening her mouth. "So this is how Zorn women do it?" She licked the harder section of skin at the top of his head.

"Yes," he groaned. "That feels so good."

"Which is better? You tell me." She opened her mouth wide to accommodate the head, then relaxed her jaw and took him deeper. She teased the underside of him with her tongue, the roof of her mouth rubbing his oversensitive spot.

Ral growled as his fingers gently massaged the sides of her head. "That is so good. I like this so much better."

Ariel gazed up at him as she released him from her mouth. "I have a better idea. I want to try something."

He arched an eyebrow. "What do you want to try?"

Using his arms, she pulled herself to her feet, laughing at his confused look. "Lie down flat on your back for me."

He climbed up on the exam table. Ariel saved the sample cup when his bare leg hit it and knocked it over the edge, as Ral eased his large body down. He turned his head when he was flat on his back. "You want to bend over me?"

She shook her head and climbed up on the table with him. "I want to try a new angle, and since I don't want you to hold me upside down, this will work." She straddled him so her ass was facing him and inched back until they were in the sixty-nine position. Her knees ended up near his armpits. Ral growled. Large hands slightly trembled as they gripped Ariel's thighs.

"Lord of the Moons, Ariel! I love this view of you." His hands slid up her thighs to spread her, one of his thumbs brushing against her clit.

Ariel moaned. "Do that. Tease me. Don't make me come though. Tell me how this feels."

She took him into her mouth. She enjoyed the hard, ridged texture of his *hais* as she moved her tongue. His pre-cum that tasted like candy. She moaned, loving his taste. She sucked on him, taking him into her mouth a little deeper, moving her tongue to draw out more of his sweetness.

The hand on her thigh tightened almost painfully as Ral groaned loudly. His body under hers tensed hard. His thumb pressed tight to her clit, frozen there, before he slid it higher and pushed the thick digit into her pussy. He fucked her with his thumb, hooking her inside to rub against her G-spot.

Ariel moaned against his cock. Ral moaned louder. She hadn't known it was possible for him to get any harder but the impossible happened. She felt how swollen and hot his cock got as she slowly teased him with her mouth. His rigid shaft had turned to the consistency of steel. She knew he wouldn't last much longer. Ral's lower stomach muscles started to quiver against her breasts. He made a sound that was close to a whimper. He jerked his thumb out of her body to grip her thighs with both hands.

She released him, turning her head and lifting her upper body to see over her ass. Ral's eyes were closed tightly and his lips was parted, his sharp teeth exposed. He looked like he was in pain.

"Am I hurting you? Oh, Ral! I'm so sorry."

His head lifted as his eyes snapped open. The blue of his eyes looked darker and seemed to have lost some of the glowing look. "It doesn't hurt. Lord of the Moons! You have to stop though. I will spill my seed. You do that and it feels so good, I have no control. I almost spent my seed, and would have if you hadn't stopped."

Relief hit her. She thought she might have hurt him. She laughed. "Too much?"

"It feels too good for words. It makes me want to come fast."

"Okay. I'll ease back more."

"No. Just be ready. I am near to losing my seed."

She reached for the small cup and licked the top of his cock as if he were an ice cream cone. Her tongue traced over the mushroomed head and he shivered under her. She eased him into her mouth once more. Using her tongue and her lips, she tugged on him in shallow pulls of suction. His hands flexed on her thighs.

Ral groaned. "Now!"

She released him from her mouth to put the cup up just in time to catch his seed. She collected a fair bit then put the top on the cup, and noticed Ral was still hard. Without hesitation, she opened her mouth and took him back inside, closing her eyes in delight. He tasted like melted cotton candy. He was better than any dessert she'd ever had.

"Lord of the Moons," Ral whispered. "Stop, Ariel. I can't take it." His large, muscular body shivered. "You make me feel so good it almost hurts."

She released him with her mouth and stood up carefully so the sample cup didn't go tumbling. Ral's face was flushed as she stepped away from the exam table. A sappy grin spread his lips as he sat up.

"I'm in love with you," he said softly. "You remind me why so often. This is one of those times."

She moved the sample to another table and turned to him, grinning. "One sample down. Where do you want me, Ral?"

He eased his body from the table and reached for her. Ariel was amazed at his strength yet again as he lifted her effortlessly into the cradle of his arms. They were almost face level. He planted a tender kiss on her lips and then stretched her out on the exam table. He released her, walking to the end of the table to grip her ankles. He grinned wickedly as he yanked her down the table until her ass was at the very edge.

"Spread wide for me."

Ariel spread her thighs and reached down, gripping her bent knees. She watched Ral's eyes take in every inch that was exposed to him. She'd been self-conscious about her body once. Not anymore. The look on Ral's face was one that always turned her on. *He* turned her on. He dropped slowly to his knees as his large hands caressed the inside of her thighs.

"I get so hard when I see you like this. You are so pink and wet for my touch. I get harder from your scent of arousal and the taste of you. You are ready for me."

"Only for you," she whispered.

Ariel closed her eyes as Ral lowered his head. He slid his rough-textured hands over her thighs and his thumbs spread her wider to his view. He hesitated for only a moment before the first touch of his tongue had Ariel moaning loudly.

Ral had no mercy. His tongue found her clit immediately. He licked at her with hard strokes and pleasure tore through her body. The man hadn't known what a clit was when they met, but he'd sure gotten down how to handle one with his mouth like a pro.

He sucked and licked. One of his hands shifted and she bucked her hips as he pushed a finger deep inside her. He pushed in another finger and twisted them to find the right spot. Ariel cried out when he found it. Ral started to pump inside her in fast movements with his fingers as his tongue teased and licked her clit.

Ariel couldn't last long with Ral. He knew too well how to touch her. She jerked under him as she climaxed but he didn't stop. His two fingers moved faster as his mouth sucked on her clit right through one of the hardest orgasms she'd ever had. He kept at her until she begged him to stop. Pleasure was turning to pain. He stopped instantly. His face lifted as he slowly withdrew his fingers.

"I want you now," he growled.

Ariel opened her eyes. She saw Ral twist around to grab one of the swab things that Ahhu had set out. He lowered his gaze to her exposed sex, used the swab quickly and put it in the sample bag, which he threw on a small table.

His hands gripped her and Ariel gasped as Ral lifted her off the table. She wrapped her arms and legs around him, the two of them nose to nose, their gazes locked.

Ral growled deep in his throat as he kissed her. It was a wild kiss, with enough passion behind it that it almost shocked Ariel. She moaned as one of his sharp fangs grazed her lower lip, then she tasted blood, which only seemed to drive Ral's passion higher. He eased one hand down between their bodies to guide his cock. The thick crown pressed against her. She knew she was soaking wet as he rubbed up and down her pussy in tight motions that teased her fervor higher .

She expected him to enter her fast and hard but he pushed into her slowly and slid deep. Ariel moaned into his mouth. He shifted his hold on her to cup her ass with both hands. He broke from the kiss to stare into her eyes.

"Tell me if I hurt you," he growled.

Ariel nodded.

Ral started to move, fast and hard, almost savage. Ariel pressed her face against his shoulder and cried out at the wonderful feeling of Ral pounding inside her. He was thick and it felt incredible as he rubbed against every nerve within her pussy. He moved even faster, driving up as his hands slammed her down on him. It didn't hurt. It felt so good her moans turned into loud sobs of pleasure.

Her body started to tense and then her mouth opened on his shoulder. She bit down, screaming against his skin as she came hard. Her interior muscles went crazy, gripping his cock tighter as Ral threw back his head. He roared out as he came, jerking violently as his semen shot inside her.

Ariel realized her teeth were still gripping his shoulder. She released him gingerly and opened her eyes. She saw her teeth marks in his skin but she hadn't made him bleed, thankfully. She lifted her gaze to meet Ral's.

He sighed. "Lord of the Moons, Ariel. Nothing compares to you."

"Wow."

"What does that mean?"

"Amazing. Wonderful. Incredible. I love you."

He laughed. His gaze lowered to her mouth and his smile faded. "I made your lip bleed. I'm sorry. It is a little swollen."

"I'm good. Don't worry about it. I bit you too. I'm just glad I didn't draw blood."

He shrugged. "I would not care if you did. It would be an honor to be marked by your teeth." His eyes went to her mouth and he smiled. "But your teeth are too smooth to damage my skin." He opened his mouth to show off his fangs. "You need a set like mine."

Ariel shook her head as she laughed. "I'd hurt *myself* if I had teeth like that."

He eased out of her body, still smiling. "We should get dressed now. I want to take you home."

"And I want to go home with you."

"No other women, Ariel. I promise this to you."

She stared up into his eyes. "You would break my heart."

"I understand. If you left me, you would break my heart as well."

Chapter Nine

The new woman was much better than the last one. Ariel smiled at the ancient Zorn female. She was still in great shape for her advanced age but she had long white hair, wrinkles galore on her face, and she wore clothing.

Erra was sweet. A broad smile had been her first reaction to seeing a human. She'd spoken words Ariel couldn't understand, since the *conis* was in the bedroom and they weren't. The older woman had slowly approached her. Ral had nodded at Ariel from the doorway with a smile to tell her it was fine.

Ariel felt so short. Every Zorn adult was a good foot or so taller than her. Even the elder Erra was at least eight inches taller. After Ral's obvious permission, the woman had wrapped Ariel in her arms, giving her the equivalent of a bear hug but without squeezing too tight. It had been startling, but Ariel had recovered enough to hug the woman back.

Erra had pulled away and then began to touch her, with Ariel standing very still as the woman's hands brushed her cheek and her hair. Staring into Erra's soft brown eyes, Ariel had seen curiosity in their depths. She got it. She was an alien, and Ral liked to tell her she was as cute as a *horma*.

A *horma* was a creature that was tiny and, to the best of Ariel's knowledge, was a little something like Zorn's version of a monkey. She wasn't sure she liked the comparison but when Ral had pulled up a photo of one on the *conis*, she'd understood. They were little blue-eyed white creatures that were, in fact, very cute. There were worse things to be compared to.

Erra loved to fuss over her, sometimes making Ariel feel like a living doll. The elder Zorn would follow her into the bedroom so they could communicate with the *conis* and, while there, Erra would always grab a hairbrush to brush out Ariel's long blonde hair. She also liked to put lotion on Ariel's exposed skin. She said that her skin was so soft, Erra was afraid it would get damaged in the dry Zorn climate.

Needless to say, Ariel felt very mothered, but she didn't really mind.

"You should remove your clothing." Erra motioned to Ariel's body. "You hide from Argis Ral." Her gaze locked with Ariel's. "Are you so different from our women to look at?"

"I like clothing. I don't sleep in it with Ral."

"Our women are naked at home. Ral would appreciate you naked. You are his bound. You have much to learn about our culture." Erra smiled at her. "He would be well pleased at the end of his day to see you naked waiting by the door. It is our custom. You should shroud your body outdoors and from other men, but never in your home."

"But I'm not Zorn, Erra. I'm not so different physically; I just don't feel comfortable walking around naked. My culture wears clothing unless they are alone with their bound for sex or sleeping or showering."

Erra sighed. "You are bound to Ral. He is Zorn. You are Zorn now."

Ariel thought about it that last statement as she walked to her closet. Ral had clothing brought to her the day they'd arrived, so she had a closet full of them, but he'd left out that the clothes were all in the equivalent of a Zorn *teenager's* size. Erra found it amusing to tease Ariel about being a lot smaller than Zorn women.

She asked the woman for something to cut with, so she could alter some of the outfits in her closet. Ariel donned one of them when she was done and eyed herself in the mirror. She was still decent—barely. She certainly was showing a lot more skin.

Most Zorn women wore loose knee-length shift dresses. If they wore bras or underwear, Ariel hadn't seen any so far. Some working women like Ahhu at the medical center wore baggy pants with tops. Ariel had limited experience with any other Zorn women. Ral kept her home. She wasn't allowed to leave the house without him.

She had cut one of the shifts high, so it was like a mini-skirt dress. She'd removed the arms and cut the front down low, exposing her cleavage. She even slit the sides a few inches so more of her thighs showed. She'd have to be careful if she sat down, since she was totally bare under the dress.

She looked good, she decided. She'd never walk outside in this getup, but she hoped Ral would like it. She wasn't ready to stroll around the house naked just yet.

When Ariel walked out of the bedroom, she smiled at Erra and slowly turned in a full circle. The Zorn woman studied her with raised eyebrows, taking in the altered dress—then she grinned. She met Ariel's gaze, raised her hand, and stuck up her thumb.

Ariel laughed, delighted when the woman used the gesture she'd taught her.

Ral worked six hours a day for four days in a row, with three days off. He was some kind of judge, as far as Ariel knew. Ral had explained that he listened to his people and dealt with their issues as fairly as he could, and he seemed to love doing it.

Ariel missed him when he was at work. Erra barely let her do anything around the house, and she wasn't allowed to leave, so that left her with either napping or following Erra around, to watch and learn what the woman did.

While she couldn't go anywhere without Ral, she *could* spend time in his backyard, which she did often. It had a pretty purple creek and black and red trees. A high wall enclosed the area. It was the only fresh air she got, so she took full advantage.

Ral avoided questions when she asked why she couldn't go shopping with Erra, or why she wasn't allowed to leave the house. He always distracted her—and the man was really good at it. He would simply carry her to bed. After a few hours with Ral, she was too worn out to question him further.

But now she stared at the clock willing the day to go faster. She'd learned to tell Zorn time quickly with Ral's help. When the little arrow hit the bird-looking symbol, he would be home.

Ariel bit her lip, wondering what would happen if she left their home. What was Ral not telling her? He *had* to be hiding something. Was she in danger from his people? Or was it was just a simple case of him worrying about her? After all, she couldn't communicate with anyone.

It had been just over a week since the medical center visit. The Zorn still hadn't perfected the Anzons' translator program to work with Zorn translators. She sighed. Maybe they had some kind of wireless, portable computers...uh, *conis*...that she could walk around with. A *conis* was about the size of a thirteen-inch TV.

She wondered if Zorn had wheelbarrows, then laughed at that idea of lugging one around with her.

The day wore on, and Ariel watched the arrow go from the bird symbol to the wiggly snake-looking one. Ral was late. She frowned. He was *always* home when the bird symbol hit.

She went in search of Erra and found the woman doing laundry. Ariel waved at her in their usual sign for "we need to talk". Erra followed her through the house.

"He's late. I'm worried."

Erra glanced at the clock. "Perhaps he went out with men. They like to drink *amond* while they talk of male bonding things."

She assumed *amond* was like beer or something; she didn't bother asking Erra explain. Men were men on any planet. "Wouldn't he have used the device to call you, to tell me he wasn't coming home?"

Erra grinned. "The males on your world do that?" She laughed. "Women rule there, do they not? The idea of one of our males asking for permission to bond with other men is funny."

Ariel sighed. "Great. So on this world, men don't call to say they'll be late?"

"No. Ral spoils you, Ariel. If other males saw the way he treats you, he would be teased unmercifully. They already talk of how he removed his two home helpers, and refused the female his father sent to bound with him. She was greatly wanted by all males. That is why she was given to Ral."

Ariel frowned.

"It is true. He refuses all females. They are attracted to him and try to entice him when he goes anywhere. He is first son, Ariel. It means he will lead this world when his father hands over the position or dies. He is very powerful and wanted. Most men in his position have at least three women in their beds, if not more. He is bound to you, but males always share sex with other women besides their bound. A bound is a male's favorite female, who he gifts with his seed. It is a deep honor to be bound. Our men have strong sexual needs that one female can never fulfill. Still, Ral refuses all but you."

"I fulfill his all needs."

Erra grinned. "I have heard."

A flush stained Ariel's cheeks. "Sorry about that."

"Do not be. You make Argis Ral very pleased. But he spoils you in this way, and in many others. Most of our females work. He doesn't want you to leave his home. He is very possessive and protective of you. I have seen him with you, and he gives you all of his attention. Our males tend to seek out attention from their bounds only during sex. Ral is always with you."

"Maybe he doesn't think there's a job I can do."

"You are very smart. There are jobs you could do where you wouldn't have to speak or be spoken to. He wants to take care of you, and keep you to himself. All bound men are possessive and protective, but he takes it to a new level. Everyone knows this."

Ariel sighed.

"You have been with Argis Ral long enough to have conceived. Did you not know that men release their bounds if those females cannot conceive? It is one of the few reasons it is allowed. But Argis Ral has no intention of giving you up. He means to keep you until death."

Ariel's anger slipped away. Ral had sacrificed for her—was *still* sacrificing. So what if he went out with the boys? He wasn't a human guy and she knew there were going to be culture differences. He'd given up a lot of his cultural beliefs already to make her happy.

She nodded. "I guess I'll play with the *conis* and try to learn more."

Erra nodded just as the doorbell went off. Ral wouldn't use it, he'd just walk in, so Erra hurried away to go see who was at the door. Ariel hesitated and then followed the woman. What if something had happened to Ral?

Fear hit her. Maybe that's why he hadn't come home.

Four large males were at the door. Erra snarled at them, and one snarled back.

Ariel hugged her body, praying the men at the door hadn't told Erra bad news about Ral. Was he hurt? Dead? Her knees wanted to buckle under her at even the thought. She loved Ral. He was her entire world. She couldn't lose him. She'd die inside if she could never be with him again, the depth of her love for him hitting home, hard.

One of the males snarled again, shifting his body, and his gaze met Ariel's.

He suddenly shoved at Erra.

She snarled viciously, trying to push the man back, but he was too strong. He shoved her hard enough that she went sprawling to the floor.

Ariel gasped and instantly took steps in Erra's direction to help her.

The three other men walked into the house—the last one slammed the door loudly behind them.

Erra hissed as her head jerked in Ariel's direction.

Ariel saw terror in the woman's eyes as their gazes locked, and it halted Ariel in her tracks. The elder Zorn snarled something at her and pointed to the bedroom, then struggled to her feet before launching herself at the man who'd knocked her down. He had started to walk toward Ariel before Erra leapt on his back, screaming her rage.

The man grabbed her arm and in one powerful motion, wrenched Erra off and sent her flying across the room to slam into a wall. Her body slumped to the floor, unmoving for a moment, but Ariel saw she still breathed. A soft moan came from the woman, then her arms moved sluggishly.

Stark fear froze Ariel in place as the four men turned their attention back to her. The one by the door grasped the front of his shirt, tearing it open. Her eyes flew to another, who reached for the front of his pants. He opened them to reveal he was erect, and it became damn clear to Ariel what they wanted as they stalked toward her slowly, leering at her body. They growled at her, softly saying God only knew what as they spaced themselves apart, trying to surround her.

Ariel screamed while she made a run for it. She must have caught them by surprise, because she made it to the bedroom and slammed the door shut behind her, locking the door. She didn't have anywhere else to go. She headed for the bathroom but turned when something hit the bedroom door—hard. The wood of the door was thick and the lock wasn't cheap, but she highly doubted either of those things would keep the men out for long.

She didn't know what to do. She was terrified. They were going to rape her, of that she was certain. They'd hurt Erra, who'd tried to defend her. She wondered fleetingly if Erra would be able to call for help, and prayed the sweet woman wasn't badly injured.

Something hit the door again and it cracked loudly. The thick wood was breaking.

Her gaze frantically searched the room. If Ral kept weapons in his bedroom, she hadn't seen them. She grabbed more clothes and hugged them to her body.

She heard loud snarls as something hit the door again and it splintered, the wood splitting in a few places.

Ariel sobbed, backing into the bathroom. She slammed the door shut and locked it. She was shaking as she quickly donned pants under her shift and tugged on one of Ral's big shirts over it. If she had to fight, she didn't want to do it mostly naked.

She frantically evaluated the bathroom. No windows. She should have tried to climb out the window in the bedroom, but it only went to the backyard. The perimeter wall was too high for her to climb and there was no gate, the walls sitting flush with the sides of the house. She would have been trapped either way. At least in the bathroom, she had one more lock door between her and those men.

When the bedroom door was breached, it crashed into the wall like a shotgun going off. Ariel yanked open drawers under the counter for a weapon. She found the *shara*, the cutting shears that Ral used to trim his hair. They were similar to extra-long scissors from back home and were wicked sharp. She grabbed them and backed up into the shower, closing the glass-like door. She had no way to lock it, but the smaller entry would hopefully mean only one man would be able to reach into the shower to grab her.

She held the shears in a death grip, prepared to use them.

They attacked the bathroom door and Ariel's heart lurched. She knew she wouldn't survive if they got their hands on her. It would be a horrible way to die. Ral was always so gentle, but Zorn men were big and really strong by nature. The four men coming after her obviously didn't care about her physical disadvantage.

She knew Ral would kill every one of them when he found out what they'd done.

As she thought of Ral, agony ripped at her. He would mourn her. She knew he loved her. She prayed he wouldn't blame himself, though she still couldn't help wishing he was there to defend her. She'd seen him fight four men before. The men who had entered the house weren't as mean looking as the ones on the asteroid, who had who'd tried to take her from him. Ral could take these assholes apart eas—

The bathroom door crashed in. Ariel's time was up.

She saw movement just before the man who'd attacked Erra yanked open the door. Shirtless now, he reached in to grab her.

Ariel screamed and, using the shears like a knife, gripping them with both hands, she threw herself forward and stabbed him in the chest.

The handles of the sheers dug into her skin from the tight grip but they didn't cut her—then she felt warm blood pour onto her hands.

She screamed again as the man roared out in pain. He staggered, the shears embedded deep in his chest.

Ariel threw herself back and hit the shower wall hard enough to knock the breath from her own lungs. She stared at the man's face as he stumbled into his companions. He looked down at the shears protruding from his chest, shock clear on his face. He went completely silent before he collapsed to his knees.

His companions were frozen in disbelief as they stared at the man whose blood was running down his chest.

The injured man pitched forward and didn't move again. The shears must have pushed in deeper when he fell because Ariel saw the sharp points of them sticking out of his back. Blood ran from the wound and over his sides to the bathroom floor.

One of his companions threw his head back, howling, followed by the others, the noise deafening.

Ariel screamed.

The three men suddenly went silent. She knew by their expressions they were going to make her suffer before they killed her. She had no doubt.

One of the men stepped over his fallen friend to reach into the shower stall, grabbing Ariel by the front of Ral's shirt. She heard material tear in his hand as he jerked hard. Her foot hit the low wall of the shower stall, pain shooting up her leg as she was yanked forward. Then she hit the dead man's body as she was dragged screaming from the bathroom.

Ariel's feet left the floor completely when the man threw her toward the bed. She hit it hard enough that it bounced her body off to the other side. She hit the floor, pain exploding in her hip, thigh and arm from the impact. Ariel saw their feet from under the bed, starting to move around it. She knew if she lay there, she'd die.

She rolled completely under. Zorn beds weren't that different from her bed at home, except they were taller and on sturdier frames. She inched to the center of the massive bed, panting, reaching up to grab the bars of the frame.

Her fingers barely had time to fight between the bars and the mattress before a large hand clamped down on her ankle.

She screamed in pain as one of the men tried to drag her out. It almost tore her hold from the bars. He'd yanked her hard enough that her feet were no longer under the bed, her arms stretched painfully above her since she refused to let go.

"Get her out of there!" one of the men snarled.

The *conis* was still on. She could understand them, so she *knew* they could understand her as well. It probably wouldn't help, but she had to try.

The hand around her ankle increased its pressure until she screamed again. It felt like he was crushing her ankle. The bastard was purposely hurting her to make her let go.

"Ral will kill you! Don't do this!"

"Ral is busy," another male snarled. "We will set fire to his house when we are done with you, there will be no scent of us left for him to track."

"Get her out *now*! We don't have much time."

The man gripping her ankle pulled harder. Ariel screamed again. Her fingers were torn painfully from the bars and the man dragged her out from under the bed. She stared up at three half-undressed Zorn males. The one gripping her ankle didn't let go, instead grabbing her pants with his other hand. He fisted them and yanked hard.

Ariel kicked at him with her free foot. Zorn males were freakishly tall, in her current opinion, since she couldn't even reach his balls. Her legs were too short. She did manage to kick his thigh, and continued screaming and fight as her pants were brutally yanked down her body. She tried to roll and grab for the bed. If she could just get away and crawl back under there, she could avoid being raped just a little longer.

The other two men bent down, grabbing each of her flailing arms. They lifted her and she found herself dropped on her back on the bed. The man holding her ankle captive put his knee on the end of the bed between her thighs.

Ariel yanked her free leg up to her chest and, with pure terror filling her, found the strength to kick at him again.

This time she nailed the man harder, and in a better place. His head snapped back as her heel slammed into his jaw. The hold on her ankle loosened, her attacker clearly suffering from the force of his head slamming back so hard. It didn't break his neck, unfortunately, because he roared out in pain.

Then Ariel heard another roar—and it sounded close.

The men holding her arms whipped their heads in the direction of the bedroom door.

Ariel didn't waste time trying to figure out what captured their attention. She was hurting. Her ankle might be broken or at least sprained, but she ignored the pain. The man at her feet was holding his jaw with one hand, still gripping her ankle with the other. Ariel jerked her foot back to her chest again. Taking aim, she kicked out as hard as she could with everything she had left.

Her foot nailed the man's crotch.

She'd hit her intended mark. She saw his mouth fly open, his hold on her ankle suddenly gone as he grabbed for the front of his pants.

He fell slowly backward and crashed to the floor, emitting a high-pitched squeal.

Joy hit Ariel for a fleeting second. Apparently that was another way men were similar, no matter what universe they came from.

She twisted her body to kick at one of the other men who held her but they abruptly released her, both of them backing away from the bed before she got her chance. Terror was etched on their faces as they stared toward the broken bedroom door. Her eyes followed theirs...

Ral stormed into the bedroom.

Rage like nothing she'd ever seen before twisted his features. He roared, the sound making her ears ache. The *conis* didn't translate, but she didn't need to be told what that primal scream meant.

Ral's gaze met Ariel's. She saw his eyes flash over her body briefly...

Then he moved fast, throwing himself at the nearest man, the attacker on Ariel's right.

Something warm sprayed her side. She looked down and saw bright red dots all over her body. Her brain registered it was blood even as her eyes turned in shock to Ral and the man.

She saw the flash of a metal blade in Ral's hand before the large intruder dropped to his knees, his throat slashed. He pitched forward, obviously dead.

Ral roared again as he dove for the other man before the first body had even hit the floor. The second man didn't get out a sound before Ral was on him, taking him to the ground, his arm with the blade raised high.

Ariel heard a wet groan—then earie silence.

It was soon broken by a soft, gasping whine from the end of the bed.

Ral rose from the floor alone. He walked slowly to the end of their bed, glaring down at the man Ariel had kicked in the crotch. He bent, his face still a mask of pure rage.

Another whine—louder this time, pleading—came from the man. Ral dragged him up by his hair, and then his hand moved lightning fast.

Ariel watched as Ral slit the man's throat.

The body was tossed aside and then Ral stood there, breathing hard. He was completely bloodstained, crimson on both of hands, dripping from the blade, and splashed on his clothes. He turned to stare down at Ariel.

"I'm okay," her voice broke. "You got here in time."

Ral dropped the blade on the bed. Ariel didn't flinch as he reached for her with two bloody hands. He gently lifted her into his arms and held her tightly against his bloody chest. He buried his face in her throat. He was still breathing hard and shaking with fury.

Ariel didn't hesitate. She threw her arms around his neck and held on to him for dear life.

Ral had saved her again. He'd killed for her again. They had survived and they were together.

Chapter Ten

Ral refused to put her down. He refused to leave her side. Ariel didn't mind at all.

He sat on the couch with Ariel firmly on his lap, Ral's arms around her, holding her tight. They were both clean after a shower, with wet hair and fresh clothing. The dead men had been removed from Ral's home.

She'd been lucky. Besides some bruises, she'd just sustained a sprained ankle. Nothing was broken.

The uniformed Zorn version of a police force had come and gone. Ahhu had arrived to treat injuries. Erra was bruised but also fine. She'd run for help but Ral had gotten home before the nearest neighbors could rush to Ariel's aid. The *conis* had been moved into the living room. The bedroom was still bloodstained and off limits until it could be cleaned.

"I don't understand why they would dare," Erra said softly. "You are Argis Ral." The woman held ice to the large bump on the side of her forehead. "It would mean death for them, whether they harmed Ariel or not."

Ral eased his hold on Ariel and gripped her jaw gently, turning her face so they could stare into each other's eyes. "I know why this happened. I know you will be angry. I am *enraged*. When we took the tests at medical, we were monitored without our knowledge. Someone with access to those recordings released them to the population to watch on the *conis*. We were seen by many."

Ariel blinked.

Then she was horrified as his words set in.

The blood drained from her face and she felt a little dizzy. Her heart almost stopped. She stared into his eyes and saw his rage reflected there. He nodded at her grimly.

"Many males probably viewed the monitoring of us. I think that is why they dared come after you. They wanted to do what they saw between us."

"Oh God," she breathed. "I'm in a porn video on the internet with you!"

He frowned. "I—"

"I know. You don't understand, but I do. What we did, anyone can see on the *conis*, right? Us, naked, doing what we did together at medical?"

"I had it removed from the archive."

"But once it's on the *conis*, isn't it out there? You can't stop it from being seen."

He frowned. "That is not true. Once it is removed from the archive it is gone from the *conis*."

"Can't someone store it and watch it later, or put it back on the *conis*?"

"Our *conis* is not like that. It has to be in the archive to enable one to view."

Relief hit her. "You're sure?"

"Positive. That is why I was late. I was told about it and had it taken care of. All monitoring of us was destroyed. It makes me burn with rage to think of the males who saw you naked! They saw what I see when I touch you. That is mine alone. I want to kill every male who looked at your beautiful body being touched by me."

She closed her eyes, opening them again after taking a deep breath. "So why did they attack? I still don't understand, especially if it would mean their deaths. Why couldn't they just do those things with their own women?"

"You are very responsive to my touch, and you are different from our women. You make males very hard, Ariel. Very hard and very stupid, if they think they can touch you and come after you. I will make them very *dead* if they try again. I have kept you home out of fear that you would attract males with your beauty. I was afraid they might scare you by approaching you to talk...but I *never* thought anyone would dare attack you. They know you are mine."

The front door suddenly opened. Ariel gasped as she was removed from Ral's lap so fast the world spun. He leapt to his feet to snarl at whoever had walked into his home, placing himself between Ariel and the front door to protect her. She could see Ral's entire body tense.

Then just as quickly, his large frame slowly relaxed. He sat back down, reaching for Ariel and lifting her back onto his lap.

She stared in shock at their company, feeling instant anxiety.

Six men entered the room. Ariel recognized three of Ral's brothers and his father. The other two men were strangers, but they dressed like some sort of guards, if the weapons strapped to their hips were any indication.

The front door shut firmly when the last male entered the room.

"What do you want?" Ral glared at his father. "I am furious with you. *You* ordered those tests. Only *you* could order us monitored without consent! What happened to Ariel is your fault!"

Hyvin Berrr slightly lowered his chin. His eyes, much like Ral's, stared back at his son. "I did not know someone would steal the monitoring feed and put it on the *conis* for all to see. That was not my intention. You are destined to take my place one day, Zorn, to lead our people. I needed to make sure you were not bewitched. I wanted her tested. I wanted to see how she was controlling you."

Ral snarled. "You put her life in danger!"

The man lowered his gaze. He glanced at the floor and then back at Ral. "I know. I have no excuse. I apologize. I know she is not bewitching you. I saw the monitoring and the test results state there is no chemical control."

"Shit," Ariel sighed. "Great. Did anyone *not* see us having sex?"

"I did not," Erra said in a very soft tone.

Ariel shot her a grateful look and a wry smile. "Thank you."

"We all saw it," Argernon said with a growl. He shot his father a cold glare. "We did not realize what we were supposed to watch, or I would have walked out of that meeting. He called us all in to evaluate what he called a 'possible threat'."

All of the color drained from Ariel's face. "Wonderful." She glanced at Ral. "So I guess everyone in your family has seen us having sex now."

He growled at his brothers and his father. "I am outraged!"

"I do not blame you," Hyvin Berrr said quietly. "I never thought it would be given to the population for viewing. I am very apologetic, Ral. It was not my intention to endanger either of you in any way. It was not my intention for any of this to happen. It was to be a private family matter. We viewed the monitoring and realized what was between the two of you was not a matter of forced control."

One of the brothers snorted. "She could control *me* if she—"

Argernon shot out a fist and hit the man speaking hard in the mouth. He growled. "That is your brother's bound woman. Respect her now!"

The younger brother winced and slapped his hand over his now-bleeding split lip. He nodded.

Argernon sighed, staring at Ral. "What father is saying is that he doesn't know how to make this right. Not only has he caused you problems with your bound, and with other males wanting her—"

"Desperately," the younger brother said around his hand.

Argernon snarled. "Keep talking if you want to lose some teeth." He spoke to Ral. "Father has really made a mess of things. That monitoring was viewed by many males, unfortunately. It has caused widespread trouble. We have no right to ask it, but need your help, Ral. We need you to set aside your rage because there is serious trouble brewing with our people."

Ral tensed. Emotions flitted across his face and his mouth pressed into a tight line. He looked pissed as he shot his father a glare before giving his brother his full attention.

"What is the problem?"

Argernon hesitated. He looked at Ariel and then back to Ral. "They want one of her. Some demand we allow them to go to her planet to find women to bound with."

Ariel knew she wasn't the only one shocked by Argernon's statement. She heard Ral suck in a harsh breath as his body tensed. He relaxed after long seconds, shaking his head no.

"Tell them we are not into slavery. What they want is wrong. We do not go to other planets to steal women. We have a good population of women right here. Our males do outnumber our females but it is not an issue."

"We tried." It was the brother who hadn't spoken yet. "They are threatening to revolt, Ral. We could have a war on our hands. If they attacked our family en masse, we would be stripped of power. Too many of them want to bring her species here. They want one like her."

"I'm not a damn toy!" Ariel was pissed off. "Ral is right. You can't go to my planet to kidnap women."

"They are not the same as our women." Ral frowned.

The younger brother snorted. "No shit." His lip had stopped bleeding. "She's built for pure enjoyment. She's way *better* than our women. It was so hot watching you do her standing up, facing each other, with her in your arms."

The father turned this time to punch the youngest son in the room, hard enough to make him stagger back.

Hyvin Berrr growled. "Enough." He turned to give Ariel an apologetic look. "He is young and his mouth is run by his lower region. Please forgive his youth."

Ral lifted Ariel from his lap and gently sat her down next to him. He slowly stood up to glare at his youngest brother. "One more word to embarrass Ariel and I will knock you out." He shot his father a glare. "They do not understand that she is different in more ways than sexually."

Hyvin Berrr hesitated. "Will you share how?"

"They do not share with others sexually." Ral's tone was quiet. He shot his youngest brother a glare. "That means only one woman to share sex with until death." He looked back at his father. "She is very conscious of her nude body. She won't walk around naked unless we are alone. It is their way. They need strong emotions from a male to have sex, and Ariel needs strong commitment and attention from me to be happy. I am content to give both—but will others do the same?"

Ral eyed the quiet brother, the one who had only spoken once. "Rever, they are very uncontrollable. I find it refreshing, but most males would take issue with a woman who will not submit on demand. Her kind resists control, from what I have learned from her. She has not conceived, so it is doubtful we will have offspring. It matters none to me. I want *her* more than anything else. I know many males demand to bound to women who can provide offspring."

Argernon finally smiled. "We will release this information. It will perhaps make them rethink wanting a female like her, no matter how interested they are sexually. It might work. Otherwise, we still will face a problem."

Rever met Ariel's gaze. "Is your world very different from ours?"

She hesitated. "The water is blue and so is the sky. We only have one moon. The trees are brown and green, for the most part. Men and women are equal. Women fought for that right—and we do love a good fight. We have a history of fighting back when we are attacked. If I didn't love, Ral you'd have serious problems with me."

"She killed one of her attackers, and injured another," Ral said in a soft voice, to the clear shock of his brothers. "They will kill to protect themselves. They are a strong people. They deserve our respect. If some of our men wish to find Earth women to bound with, it must be voluntary on the female's part."

"Agreed," Hyvin Berrr growled. "We will give them the facts of your female's species. We will demand that if any wish to attempt to bound one, they must gain the female's permission—and do so without alerting her world of our existence." The man looked at Ariel. "Do your people know of us?"

"We think we're alone in the universe. We suspect and hope that other people exist on other planets, but...I don't know if we're ready for someone to openly visit. It would make them afraid, and my people are dangerous when they're afraid. Most would attack what they fear. My planet is divided by many leaders and not all of them are of the same mind. They frequently have fights between them that turn into wars. I think they would attack you if they knew you were on our planet. We haven't the technology yet to travel too far into space. We're getting there, though. One day, perhaps, but I don't think my people are ready for first contact with your race."

"What would you suggest?"

She hesitated, staring at Ral. She loved him. He was everything to her. If some of his men were willing to love one of her kind as much as he loved her, who was she to stand in the way?

She looked at Ral's father. "Do you swear you'll ensure the women have to agree to leave with your men?"

"I swear."

"Then stick to the most remote areas to find women, and don't allow my people to know you're even there. You'd have to hide your visit. We have great communications systems, with portable devices to call for help if need be. We have mechanical eyes in space that track movement around our planet. And we have a lot of weapons.

"I'd suggest taking small spaceships and landing only after darkness falls. There have been tons of sightings of spaceships at night in remote areas of the world. Most people just think others are crazy when they claim to see one. No one really takes it that seriously…unless someone has proof. Don't give them any. We also speak many different languages. I speak English. Since we're sure the Anzon program translates my language, finding other women who speak it is a good idea, to be sure you can communicate with them. I'm from the United States."

"We'll work it out." Hyvin Berrr nodded at his son. "I made this mess, and I will clean it up, Ral. I have set guards around your home to protect your bound. I have asked Rever to take your duties for a few weeks so you can bond with your bound and soothe her from the trauma that happened here today. I never meant her harm. You have my deepest apology, my son. Somehow I will make this up to you."

Ral sighed. "You accept Ariel as my bound?"

Hyvin Berrr bowed low. "I do, my son." He stayed bowed and looked at Ariel. "You are to remain bound to my son. I give you my apology as well."

"Thank you," Ariel whispered.

"You could make this up to us by making it a priority to integrate the translation program from the Anzons into our translation implants. I would like to be able to communicate with Ariel at all times, not just in a room with the current program running on the *conis*."

Hyvin Berrr nodded. "Consider it a priority. I will inform medical to put all their staff on it before the day is over."

"Thank you, Father. Thank you for the guards as well to help me protect Ariel."

Ral pulled Ariel against his body. He was silent as his family and the guards left. Ariel smiled at Erra as the woman quietly got up and walked through the kitchen to her bedroom, which was on the other side of the house. Ariel and Ral ended up alone in the living room. He sighed.

"My family made a mess of our lives."

Ariel snorted. "That's something humans and Zorn have in common. Families can screw up big time when they think they're doing the right thing by putting their noses in someone's business."

He frowned. He opened his mouth.

She laughed. "I know. I lost you. It's a universal thing for families to try to protect who they love, and make a bigger mess of it in the process."

He grinned. "Humans do this as well?"

"Oh yes." She grinned back at him, but her smile fell with her next thought. "How many of your people do you think saw us having sex?"

He shrugged. "I am sorry the monitoring was put on the *conis*, but it is done. We have no way of changing that."

"At least your father accepted us."

"If I knew that was all it would take, I would have invited him to watch us have sex. Since we returned, he has been shoving females at me while I was at work to try to lure me from you. It has angered me greatly."

"You never said anything."

"Would you have wanted me to leave? I have a job to do."

"You don't have a job for a few weeks. You heard your father. He's making your brother cover your duties."

A grin split Ral's face. "That means we can be alone, and you will stay naked for me." He stood up, swinging her into his arms, and started to walk toward the bedroom. He froze. Again, Rage crossed his features. "Our room has been violated."

"The guestroom."

He nodded. "Tomorrow I will have the room stripped of everything and made whole. We will make it our room again."

She wrapped her arms tightly around his neck. "I love you, Ral."

He tilted his head to kiss her, his eyes sparkling. "I love you, Ariel. I am about to love you for many hours."

Chapter Eleven

Ariel was nervous, but she didn't know what anyone could really do for her. She stared at Ral, who actually looked frightened. He gripped her hand.

"If they have no help for you, we can have you back on your planet in a week. I contacted my father. He had someone study the Anzons' charts with the description you gave me of your world. We think we have found Earth. It would be a week of fast travel, but I would get you there so your medical can look at you. I won't allow you die, Ariel! You are everything to me."

Ariel fought tears. She felt ugly. She had a fever. She was a blotchy red, like she'd gotten a mild sunburn. She was also experiencing swelling. It was like PMS symptoms but worse. Her stomach was bloated, her breasts ached, and her fingers were swollen.

"I don't think this is going to kill me. I think I'm having some kind of allergic reaction. I probably ate something that caused it."

He softly growled. "You are suffering. I hate that you do not feel well. Your skin is hot like mine; it is usually so much cooler. And I know your breasts hurt. You keep pulling your shift away from them and you get an irritated look on your features."

She smiled at him. "Do you normally watch me that closely?"

He smiled back. "You always have my full attention when you play with your clothing...or remove them."

Ahhu was the medical personnel permanently assigned to Ariel. She was the best in her field and took care of the entire Berrr family. She walked in smiling.

Ariel relaxed on the exam table. If Ahhu was smiling after running all those tests on her, then it must be something they had a cure for.

"Lean back and go flat," Ahhu ordered Ariel. "I have found the cause of your discomfort. This is a first, so we have to watch you very closely, but I think you will be fine."

Ariel eased down onto her back. Ahhu flicked a switch and a screen came to life on the wall, then she opened a cabinet under the exam table. She retrieved some kind of long, thin wand. She smiled again as she lifted Ariel's shift.

Ariel almost protested as the woman shoved up her dress, revealing the naked lower two-thirds of her body. Ahhu waved the wand over Ariel's stomach.

"Look." Ahhu pointed at the screen.

Ariel stared at the shadows and colors on the screen. It looked like green mist with a darker shape.

She heard Ahhu chuckle. "Do you see what I see?"

"Green. That's what I see." Ariel shot Ral a look. "Do you know what she's talking about?"

He shook his head and growled at Ahhu. "What is it?"

Ahhu actually *giggled*, clicking something on the wand. She set it down and walked to the frozen screen. "See this dark mass here? There is the head. Here is the body. There is an arm...and these are the bent legs." She grinned at them. "You are successful at breeding."

Shock hit Ariel. She stared at the screen and saw the shape of a baby there, now that it was pointed out. Tears fill her eyes.

She had cried last week when they'd implanted her with a working set of translators in her ears. She'd thought *that* was the best news she'd ever get from medical. Her gaze flew to Ral.

He was staring at the screen in shock. His mouth had dropped open.

He snapped it shut, swallowed hard—then threw his head back and let out a roar.

It made Ariel jump, it startled her so badly. She stared at Ral after he stopped with the ear-splitting roar. His grin was almost painfully wide. Excitement and happiness were crystal clear in his eyes as he looked at Ariel.

"We have made an offspring together!"

She laughed and cried. "We have. Oh, Ral. I love you!"

Ral kissed her gently, but then he lifted his head and his smile faded. He growled at Ahhu. "Is she in danger? She isn't well. If the offspring risks her life, you must save Ariel. She is the most important thing to me."

Fear hit Ariel. She hadn't thought of that. She turned her head. The woman smiled again.

"Do not worry, Argis Ral. I have run many tests. The baby is healthy and strong. I believe that she is feverish because *our* bodies run hotter, so your offspring is making her warmer than normal. She is in no danger. We will cool her body down a little. It will help her color and her body heat will return to a more normal temperature. We will monitor her very closely. The bloating is normal with our women. It is the body's way of making sure it retains plenty of fluids." She looked at Ariel. "Your offspring-carrying women do not do the same?"

Ariel frowned. "I don't think so. I've heard of swelling late in pregnancy. Uh, carrying offspring. How far along am I? Can you tell?"

Ahhu nodded. "Two moon cycles."

Two months. Ariel smiled. "And how many moon cycles do your females carry offspring inside them? On my planet it's nine."

"Eight."

Ral sighed in relief. "So it is not that different?"

Ahhu smiled. "I'm sure it will be fine. You breed. That means we are compatible. This is good news. Your father will be thrilled, Argis Ral."

Ral chuckled. "He's always wanted one of his sons to have offspring. You will be very spoiled by him, Ariel. Be prepared."

Ariel laughed. "We'll make a list of things he can give us."

Ral winked. "Ask for me to have more time from work."

It was Ahhu's turn to laugh. "I will leave you alone. I must make your father aware. This means that human women are breeding compatible. For any males who would like to bound with humans, this will be a joyous occasion as well." She fled the room.

Ral lowered Ariel's shift down her body and lifted her into his arms, sitting down on the table with her on his lap. He studied the screen with their baby still displayed there.

"We have it all now, Ariel. I am the happiest man on Zorn."

Ariel wrapped her arms around his neck and wiggled on his lap. Ral's cock hardened under her ass. He always wanted her. "We do have it all. And I am the happiest *woman* on Zorn."

Ral stood, holding her close to his chest. "Let's go home. I want to show you my love."

She chuckled. "Walk fast."

Made in the USA
Middletown, DE
17 October 2016